TUMBLEWEED

TUMBLEWEED

Stories

Josip Novakovich

ESPLANADE BOOKS
THE FICTION IMPRINT AT VÉHICULE PRESS

Published with the generous assistance of the Canada Council for the Arts, the Canada Book Fund of the Department of Canadian Heritage, and the Société de développement des entreprises culturelles du Québec (SODEC).

Esplanade Books editor: Dimitri Nasrallah
Cover design: David Drummond
Photo of author: Benjamin Dobutovic
Typeset in Minion and Gill by Simon Garamond
Printed by Marquis Printing Inc.

LIBRARY AND ARCHIVES CANADA CATALOGUING IN PUBLICATION

Novakovich, Josip, 1956-, author
Tumbleweed / Josip Novakovich.

Short stories.
Issued in print and electronic formats.
ISBN 978-1-55065-451-6 (paperback). – ISBN 978-1-55065-457-8 (epub)

I. Title.

PS3564.O925T84 2017   813'.54   C2016-902048-7
C2016-902049-5

Published by Véhicule Press, Montréal, Québec, Canada
www.vehiculepress.com

Distributed by LitDistCo
www.litdistco.ca

Printed in Canada on FSC certified paper

For my wandering son and daughter, Joseph and Eva,
and to strays, who would prefer a few scraps of food than words,
but they'll get that too.

CONTENTS

Tumbling: Belgrade

The town in which I grew up, Daruvar, was divided along many lines: believers and non-believers, communists and anti-communists, Serbs and Croats (and Czechs), but these were all superficial divisions. The really deep and substantial one was between alcoholics and non-alcoholics. I was informed early on that I belonged to the non-alcoholic camp. My father, mother, and siblings—none of them drank. It was a little different with my uncles, one of whom fell off a barn after drinking plum brandy and broke his neck, and another who kept a vineyard and was always flush-faced, quiet, and jovial, selling suits in the centre store. Into my late teens, I didn't drink at all, and I avoided some of my friends who did. They got together, drank beer and brandy, and passed out. Others went to village fairs, got drunk, ended up in fistfights, and had sex with village girls in haystacks.

Most were amateur drunks; a friend of mine, a few years older than me, informed me that alcoholism was a disease, first defined as such by the United States in 1956, coincidentally my birth year. Previously, alcoholism was a phenomenon, now it was a disease. Pop (my friend) explained to me that there were all sorts of alcoholics, such as *rakijasi* (brandy drinkers), *pivasi* (beer drunks) and, worst of all, *vinasi* (winos). Something in wine hooked these people incurably. I said, I don't know any winos. Oh, you can recognize them easily, said Pop. They dehydrate, so when you see a man drink several glasses of water in the morning, you might look for the correlation of wine in the evening and water in the morning. Nobody needs to drink water in the morning except alcoholics, he claimed.

However, winos were not all that bad, it turned out. Namely, when I needed to visit Belgrade to take a TOEFL (Test of English as a Foreign Language) so I could apply to American colleges, I said to Pop, I can't afford a hotel in Belgrade. Do you know where I could crash for the night before my test? No problem, Pop replied. I know a wino who has a little house in Zemun just outside Belgrade, with excellent bus links to the centre. How do I get in touch with him? Should I go to the post office and call him? Oh no, he's always home. I'll give you the address. Just go there, bang on the door—he's hard of hearing—and say you are Pop's friend, and give him a one-litre bottle of red wine. You'll be his best friend right away. And you can sleep over. Now, maybe he'll be in a good phase, maybe not. His father is an officer, so he's protected, but still, now and then the police, who hate winos like him, come over and slap him. For a while they came every morning and woke him up by slapping his face and kicking him. His father probably sent them to do that.

I followed Pop's instructions. It was a snowy and windy day in February. I came to a triangular square, found the little house with two shattered windows, and banged on the door. Misho opened the door, tall, dishevelled, with somewhat purple undersides to his eyes. I introduced myself, and he laughed, Josip, like Byeli. You must be Croatian, he said, as though everybody loves Byeli in Serbia and nobody would name children after him. Oh, and what do I see, a bottle of red. Yes, I replied, Plavac from Peljesac, Zinfandel from the Peljesac Peninsula. Pop says I can spend the night here. I have to take tests at the American Embassy tomorrow. At the American Embassy! Misho replied. By all means.

We sat down and lit a petroleum lamp. I haven't paid for the electricity in a year, so the city cut me off, he explained. The petrol fumes and smoke drifted, while he popped open the bottle and drank straight from it for a long while, finishing half. Good, now we can talk, he said. If you're tired, you can go right to bed. Use that down cover.

I shivered as the snow blew through the windows into the room and the wind whistled cheap melodies over the shards of glass. Misho walked to the cupboard, yanked a glass door open, and took out a handgun. Do you want to check it out? he asked. No, I'm fine here, I said. It's really cold; I don't want to leave the bed. It's an interesting gadget, he said. My grandfather had an argument one day with my grandma. She was in bed just where you are, in the same bed, at midnight, like now; it's midnight, isn't it? We haven't changed the furniture here since World War One. And he shot her. Yes, my friend, he killed my sweet grandma right there, with three bullets.

He sobbed, and threw the handgun to the floor. He drank more wine, the snow blew through the cracked windows, and I shivered. Would you like a sip? Misho asked. We need more wine, this is such damn good Croatian wine. No, thank you, I replied. Somehow, at that point I passed out and slept.

I woke up at dawn, found Misho asleep in the armchair, covered with a large green officer's overcoat, with a couple of shoulder stripes, probably his grandfather's from World War One, and I walked out into the biting wind, stepped onto the bus, and soon I was at the American Embassy. The administrators all smiled, displaying their enviably white teeth, and gave me a B2 pencil, to shade the ovals of the correct answers. They all drank water and I eyed them suspiciously.

Tumbleweed

leepy from spending a night at a truck stop near Rapid City, I stood on the shoulder of Interstate 90, sticking my thumb up. My arm began to hurt, and after an hour or so I sat on the side of the road, propping my arm on my backpack. Two hours later I lay on the shoulder and lifted my right leg, barefoot, sticking up my large toe.

I was standing up when a pickup braked; its tires squealed and smoked, painting grey asphalt black. I climbed into the truck, and faced a drooping blond moustache and weathered skin under a leather hat with a snakeskin brim. A black gun on the seat made me shrink back; I didn't shut the door behind me.

"What you waiting for? You aren't an Iranian, are you?"

"No." My feet crunched through a bunch of empty cans and stepped on a hunting rifle.

"At first sight, I thought you were. I'm not gonna stop for some Iranian shithead. But then I thought, so what if he's an Iranian, I could blow his brains out—do a service to the world—but you aren't Iranian?"

"No, I'm glad to say."

"Have a beer then. Name's Mike. Where you going?"

"New York."

"That's a sick town. If I was you, I wouldn't go there. I could take you to Iowa, to I-80, how would that be?"

"Tremendous," I said.

"I'm driving to Missouri, to visit my ol' man. It's lonely down there so I'm taking him a toy." He pointed to a grey snowmobile in the back of the pickup.

"It's summer," I said.

"So what? Soon it'll be winter. For old folk time passes fast. But for us fuckers on this freaking road, it's different. Man, I hope you're fun because I hate being bored."

I glanced at the gun.

"Oh, this thing, don't worry about it, it's for rattlesnakes. Hypnotizes them. Just keep it circling in front of their eyes, their heads follow. Once the sucker's got the rhythm, you pull the trigger. Head busts like a tomato. Thirsty?" He offered me another can.

I slid my thumbnail beneath the pull tab, and the smell of yeast popped out. For a while we didn't speak. On one side of the road a field of wavy alfalfa seemed to spin clockwise; on another, a field of Angus cows rotated counter-clockwise. Not all the cows faced the wind.

Brown clouds of dust made the horizon hazy. Dry, round tumbleweed, like the skeletons of globes, bounced over the road and collected along the fences.

"What are these bushes?"

"You've got an accent. Where did you say you were from? You aren't from Iran?"

"I didn't say I was from anywhere. Yugoslavia."

"How do you like it here? Much better than Czechoslovakia, isn't it?"

"I imagine it is."

"I've never been to Czechoslovakia . . ."

"Neither have I."

"Man, don't you joke like that with me, you just told me you're a Czecho."

"Yugoslav."

"Well, how'd you get out?"

"Simple," I said. "Cut the electrical wires with a pair of scissors, swam across a river into Austria. Took hot gunfire the whole way." I thought about pulling up the sleeve of my T-shirt to pass off my smallpox vaccination scars as bullet wounds.

"At least in this country we have democracy," he said.

I looked over at the speedometer as he spoke. It trembled around ninety.

"Don't worry," he said. "I don't believe in cops. Dig me a beer out of the cooler. Grab one for yourself."

We drank more than a case of beer, and then stopped for refreshments at a dark country bar and had a couple of shots of Jack Daniels. He kept laughing that he was on the road with a commie "from Yugoslavakia." "It's pretty cold in Yugoslavakia, isn't it?"

"No, Yugoslavia's on the Mediterranean," I said. Or used to be, I might have added.

"Oh, the Russians have got so far." He took off his hat, wiped his white forehead with a red handkerchief. About half a dozen Minnesotans at the bar insisted that I have a double shot of vodka, so I wouldn't feel too far away from home.

Back in the pickup, the sunlight was unbearably bright. Hawks floated on the updrafts over grassy pastures nursing placid ponds. The grey and the blue of the sky winked at us from the ponds. A hawk dove into the grass, and slowly and heavily rose from it, with empty talons.

He swallowed a white pill and gave me one too. "Amphetamines, a good invention, helps you drink more." A black Corvette passed us. Mike sped up to 110 mph and, passing the Corvette, made the international "fuck you" sign to the driver. "Nobody passes me, I mean, nobody. Not even a cop car gets by with that shit."

"Have you ever gotten a ticket?" I asked him. Instead of answering, he opened his right palm; I popped open a can and placed it in his hand.

16

"So how come you don't got no wheels?" he asked me, sympathetically, perhaps imagining that I was stripped of my license for driving.

"Too much time at school," I said. "Hoped I'd save some money this summer, working the oil fields, except I couldn't find enough work. I'd heard you could make tons here."

"You should've run into me before. I run rigs up in Montana. What work can you do?"

"Just a worm."

"That's O.K.—you could make a derrick man pretty fast if you aren't scared of heights. A little overtime, you'd be cracking fifty grand a year. I make about eighty grand, more than a fucking dentist in L.A."

"It must be a great feeling. All that money."

"Better than getting laid."

"I couldn't compare. I haven't got laid since Ford was president and I haven't ever made real money."

"Shit, as a drummer in Chicago, I got puss every night with a different woman—sometimes two, three at a time. We'd go into a hotel room, smoke weed, and bang! I screwed more in a year than a hundred average men in their lives. You'll never lay as many women as I did, I don't care how much education you got."

A green and white IOWA sign loomed huge above us. A small black and white sign appeared on the side of the road—"Speed limit 55. Mobile homes 50."

"So you study in New York?"

"Yeah, Columbia."

"Don't crap me. That's a school for rich kids—all you got is your dick, which you don't use."

"I do study there, what can I say? The rich kids are the undergrads."

"So you think you're smart? Can't get laid, can't do better than

17

work as a worm." He laughed. "A pinko at Columbia, you tell that to my gran'ma, not me!"

For a while we didn't talk. Then he said, "Well, I'm gonna crash somewheres around here, I don't know about you, but I'm wasted. Why don't you get out here? He braked suddenly and swerved on the shoulder and nearly into the cornfields.

"I thought you'd get me to 1-80," I said.

"Out!" he said.

I had barely enough time to get my backpack out of the pick-up bed. My notebook fell out and slid under the snowmobile. The pickup started quickly, the tires shooting gravel and soil in low trajectories twenty yards down the shoulder. The red sun was sinking into the cornfields. I realized my notebook was gone, and with it my novel of two hundred pages, a romance of sorts, which I was sure would be published.

Unsteady, I stuck my thumb up and looked around. A green LEMARS sign with a couple of rusty holes from bullets; a low and long building, like half a dozen mobile homes strung together—a sign that read MOTEL; a CONOCO gas pump along with junked cars and a greasy repair shop.

A truck siren hooted at me like a lonely freight train, as if I hadn't calculated there was enough time for me to cross the road to the gas station, where I asked whether there was a bus stop around so I could get up to 1-80. The attendant ignored me while pumping gas into a large Chevy.

"Is there a bust . . . eh, bus stop around here?"

No answer, so I shouted, "Are there any Christians around here?"

The husky gas attendant looked at me. "Christians? Listen, man. If you don't leave the premises pronto, I'm gonna call the cops. They'll tell you about Christians."

I was drunker than expected. "But, you must know Christ's teachings. He may even be your Lord, your personal Saviour?"

"Get lost, ya hear!" shouted the man, while a Chevy-load of sunflower faces looked at us.

I staggered into the motel and asked for the bus terminal— three miles down the road; a little too far for me. Then I asked about a single room for the night: twenty ninety-five; a little too much for me.

Stepping out, I was blinded by bright lights. I missed the last step, sank, jolting my back with its slipped disk, an accident from a construction company job. There were two police cars. Three or four cops with beer paunches stepped out of the darkness beyond the headlights. Not happy with the limelight, I sidled sideways.

"Sir, stay where you are. There's been complaints about you."

"About me? How do you know it was about me?"

"Driver's license, please?"

"But I'm not driving."

"I need it to identify you."

"I've got a green card."

"No driver's license." The cop's tone made it sound like grounds for execution. "We've got to test you. Drunk as a skunk, seems to me."

"I don't want to be tested. I am drunk, isn't that good enough? Isn't the freedom to get drunk at the root of democracy? Pursuit of personal happiness is guaranteed by the Constitution."

"Come now, it'll be better for you. Close your eyes. Bring the tip of your index finger to your nose."

"I don't want to, I *am* drunk, and so what? I'll bet you have one or two yourself now and then, when you get home after a dull day of work, with your wife in pyjamas."

"Bring that finger to your nose!" The cop was shouting now. The other one clanked a pair of handcuffs melodiously. So I followed orders, and it seemed to me I did a pretty good job, damn near hitting my nose, and only once my right eye, so that my eyeball hurt, but not badly.

"All right, now walk the straight line—put one foot right in front of the other." I did that too, and didn't fall, so I thought I must have done well there too. My assessment of the test results must have differed from theirs: they cuffed my hands, and two cops shoved me into a car. They turned on the siren and drove me around the town several times to brag about having caught a menace to law and order. I felt honoured. That was attention, certainly more of it than you get standing on the shoulder of the road for hours, passed by all sorts of people.

They led me into a police station, doing a pretty good imitation of TV scenes of cops escorting robbers. In a room, a thin investigator sitting behind the desk asked me to empty my pockets. He examined all the things on the table, one by one, as if he hadn't seen the likes of them before. He found my registered-alien card especially fascinating, though for my part I didn't think much of my photo; I had a large pimple right on the tip of my nose from unbearable heat in Miami, where I had immigrated.

He asked me what I was doing in Iowa, and I told him I was a part of the labour force in retreat. We were defeated near Laramie, Wyoming, because of the oil glut, no doubt an Iranian swindle. My anti-Iranian comment didn't seem to placate him. He asked, "Didn't you know it was illegal to be intoxicated in public?" I said I didn't. "Didn't you know it was illegal to hitchhike in Iowa?"

"But how else are you going to get around if you can't afford a car? That's discrimination against the poor."

"None of our business. We're not the welfare department. For your own good, to protect you and others, we'll put you in jail for the night, until you sober up." He now talked in a friendly voice, like a doctor sending a patient to a hot-springs spa in the Alps for a cure against rheumatism. That made me feel pretty good, thinking I'd have a free night.

"And in the morning, you'll have to go to court and pay a fine."

"A fine? I hardly have any cash, I just have this cheque from working on coal-mine silos in Wyoming . . ."

"Maybe you can get someone to wire you money," he said, turning my student ID over and cleaning his nails with it. Now I felt humiliated and hurt. So far my emotions hadn't been involved, and it all seemed sort of fun, so much bustle and bright activity, but now on account of thirty bucks, tears welled up in my nose so that I sniffed and sniffled, clearly under severe emotional strain. Another cop came by and said, "Give me your belt and shoelaces."

"Shoelaces?"

"So you don't kill yourself."

"I'm not depressed," I said. "Besides, my shoelaces are rotten." To demonstrate, I tugged at one, which instantly snapped. "See, you couldn't even hang a cat with these." But there was no arguing; I had to surrender my shoelaces.

Holding my biceps, a cop led me into an empty cell. Neon light emanated from the edge of the ceiling. The faucet water was hot; I couldn't drink it to alleviate my dehydration and headache. Even though the stool was hot too, I sat on it and remained in that philosophical attitude for hours, as if posing for a postmodern replica of a gloomy Rodin. Then I lay on a hard wooden bench in the middle of the room—I guess it was supposed to function like a bed—and tried but failed to sleep. I was nauseous; my bones, eyes, and numerous unidentified internal organs hurt.

When it seemed it must be at least noontime of the following day, I began to bang against the metal door, staring through the little barred window. Soon some other admirable citizens joined me, and we hollered, screamed, and kicked the doors of our respective cells. I hurt my toe kicking the door and wondered whether I could sue the U.S. government for compensation.

After a quarter of an hour of that jam session, a guard appeared and asked us what we wanted. We all wanted to drink and to eat. The guard brought us some frosty donuts with orange juice. The doughnuts were sticky and the orange juice tasted of flour.

A guard led me into the courthouse, a large room with some kind of wood panelling. A woman showed up in a black gown, took a small polished wooden hammer and banged with it on the table and asked me to raise my hand and swear. I had to keep my right arm raised; my left was employed in keeping my trousers from sliding down. The cops had forgotten to give back my belt. Given the appearances of most of the cops and the judge, belts were not a necessity in Iowa, where most pants looked like they would burst any minute. The judge asked me whether I was guilty of public intoxication.

"I am not guilty. It's pretty natural to be drunk."

"Answer my questions straight, to avoid further inconvenience."

She repeated her question. She seemed persistent, so I agreed to plead guilty, to get out of the tiresome place. I had to pay thirty bucks to a cashier—a cheerful woman behind the glass partition who slid me half a dozen papers to sign, with the joy and generosity of a person distributing prizes after a golf tournament. I varied my signatures to break the monotony.

I got back my belt and my shoelaces. I tried to pass the tip of the shoelaces through the appropriate holes in my sneakers. My hand trembled from the hangover, and I couldn't do it, like an old man who cannot pass a thread through the eye of a needle. A policeman observed my struggles, and I looked at him angrily. With my saliva I twisted the ends of my shoelaces into points between my forefinger and thumb—the faithful thumb that had got me so many places—and passed the laces through the holes.

It was cloudy, humid and awfully bright outside, so that the streets glared as if coated with ice. I got to the Greyhound bus terminal, bought a gallon of spring water, and sat, gulping the water loudly and waiting for a bus to Sioux City. An old man sat next to me and started chatting, "How much rain did we get last night?"

"I have no idea."

"Not enough, not enough. I sure hope it rains some more."

Since I didn't look worried about the sub-moisture of Iowan soil—I had enough worries about my own sub-moisture—the old man scrutinized me, and concluding I was an alien, asked, "How long are you staying here?"

"Half an hour longer, just passing through," I said.

"Oh, that's too bad. Our town is small, but we got some things worth seeing—the most beautiful courthouse in the whole state of Iowa. Its interior is panelled in polished oak. Just beautiful." His voice had become gruff from local patriotism. "But of course, you wouldn't have seen that." I stood up, shaking hands with the fellow-drunk, and then climbed onto a steely bus, where about a dozen babies screamed for milk (and maybe for beer and speed).

Through the tinted glass, I beheld quite a sight before the I-80 exit: a mobile home lay atop a crushed pickup, and an intact grey snowmobile stood beside them, like a faithful dog waiting for its drunk master to get up from the ditch.

Easy Living

"Villa to house-sit in Westchester County . . ." I gazed at the note on the bulletin board, jotted down the number, and rushed off to the first phone booth I could find.

Soon I was sitting in a sun-illuminated room, a toy-factory office, above the creeping traffic of Broadway's toy cars, facing the company's president, Mr. Gernhardt, who had placed the ad. Behind him was a large board with framed pictures of him shaking hands with three successive presidents, with some warm words from each written slantedly in black ink across the bottoms of the photographs in barely legible handwritings: gratitude for generous support. Mr. Gernhardt was a tall, blond, balding man with a goatee that made him look like a careful musician, a cellist rather than a fortune builder. His handshake was soft, his gaze pointed and analytical. We sat down opposite each other.

"Will you be able to stand the solitude?"

"Of course, I'd write and read. Solitude excites my imagination." I was thrilled—he spoke as if it had been settled I would house-sit; obviously, a quick judge of character. He had invested his support in the right candidate for the last three presidents, and now he clearly knew the right candidate for his house-sitter post. I hadn't brought along a resume but only a report in a college alumni magazine that I had won an arts fellowship.

"Good, I like that. So, you'll be the resident artist. Much better for you than Yaddo. Have you heard of Yaddo?"

"No."

"You will, if you stay in the business."

"And what would my duties be?"

"You should water the plants, and make sure that when it's cold the water runs overnight, so the pipes don't burst."

"Is that all?"

"Yes. And do you have a green card?"

I pulled out my green card, which was blue, whereupon Mr. Gernhardt lowered his whitish brow a bit. Maybe he could have found more use for me if I had been an illegal alien.

"Good. And if by any chance I come up there—there is a low likelihood of that in the winter—you just stay out of my way." He stood up and we shook hands as if a peace treaty had been signed.

I took a ride up to Bedford, in the country, with his personal secretary, a Filipino student of computer science. To kill time we chatted, and he told me how scandalized he was that American college students knew so little about math. I said I saw no reason why students should know the absurd definitions, that parallel lines meet in infinity rather than nowhere, that the square root of -1 is an imaginary number. He looked at me with respect, as if these little bits proved that I knew math. But I could infer that his real opinion of me had been, and maybe still was, that I was a total idiot, incapable of anything but house-sitting.

We drove through snow, which made the place look like a land of puritan innocence (especially after the burnt-out South Bronx), and made many turns, and all the roads looked alike.

"It looks kkkomplicated," said the Filipino, "but once you get used to it, you'll find your way here no problem."

The house sat halfway under the ground, with large glass windows and stone floors. Heat came from the floors, as well as from the roof, atop which sat a solar energy panel. The luminous house was in the middle of the woods; you couldn't see the road from it, even though the trees were bare.

Soon I was left there alone, master of the domain. My room was bright; one oak tree stood outside of it. I set my typewriter on the solid-oak writing desk.

It was pleasant to be able to sleep as much as I wanted, wrapped in crisp clean sheets; drive around, buying bluefish and baking it with butter and garlic. I even had use of the Jacuzzi, where I read *Jude the Obscure*. My *Obscure* fell into the water several times and was all wrinkled, so I had to buy another one. I hit it off with the bookstore girl, a Wellesley punk dropout with multi-coloured hair. We sat in the Jacuzzi together whenever she visited. Her gaze was always distant and hazy. She was unhappily in love with a Japanese man—a John & Yoko story—who no longer wrote to her. While making love with her eyes closed and nostrils flaring, she probably visualized me as Japanese.

Occasionally I had friends visit me from New York. I prepared good food for them, but we had to be very careful, lest we should damage the shiny mahogany table, which interfered with our good time. Strong beams of light illuminated the pond, inviting a tribe of raccoons, who waited humbly and insistently for the leftovers. The wives of my friends threw them the best parts of my bluefish, exclaiming, "Mark, look, this one's a baby! How sweet!" And the dozen raccoons soon snorted at each other, defending their morsels fiercely. After dinner, we sat naked in the sauna pouring water over coals, while drinking chilled Heinekens.

Christmas came. Mr. Gernhardt called up and said that his plans to take a trip to Tahiti had fallen through, so he would spend ten days in Bedford. His cook drove him up in a Mercedes coupe with a middle-aged lady, both of them smelling like some exotic flowers and disinfecting chemicals. The lady was of unremarkable appearance; however, she wore brilliant earrings and rings, and rubies, which matched her dark red hair. I was surprised that Mr. Gernhardt, a handsome divorcé, hadn't found a more attractive cohort, but after he introduced me—"This is Ms. DuPont"—it became clear what her allure might be.

They had many things to unload and, quite naturally, I helped them. The lady felt tired, and went upstairs to take a brief nap, and Mr. Gernhardt called me aside, and whispered to me, "Could you do me a big favour?"

"Well, let me hear what the favour is, before I say yes."

"You know, she's an illustrious lady, and to make a good impression on her, could you help me? . . . I know you'll think it's corny . . . but could we pretend that you are my butler? Just for the holidays?"

I like leisure but hate humiliation, so I was hard put. However, since there was nobody around, I thought I could suffer it; after all, you cannot expect to get everything for absolutely nothing . . . car, money, a villa. I said, "I guess that won't be too hard."

"But it's not that simple. Have you ever worked as a waiter?"

"Of course not."

"You call yourself a writer and haven't worked as a waiter. Well, let me tell you, that's a *sine qua non* in American letters: you must know table manners."

"But not if you write about poor people . . ."

"Poor people are out. That's no longer the style, not even with Democrats. If you want to get anywhere, you must study the manners, read *Town & Country*."

So, in other words, he expressed the whole thing as a big favour to me.

The Chinese cook appeared noiselessly and Mr. Gernhardt said, "Observe him, he'll show you how to do everything right."

I had to imitate him, placing the mats or whatever they are called on the table, soup spoons, ice-cream spoons, salad forks, crab forks, and so on, in the right places; I had to practice pouring wine with a sudden twist in the wrist, so no wine would flow over the neck down onto the label, like some bloody trickle. I was given a starched white shirt, a jazz club-type of tie, and before I knew it I was standing at the door of the dining room like a prim and stiff waiter, staring at the elegant guests. By now there were several younger couples. The smell from the kitchen spread: crabmeat, steamed asparagus, garlic and melted butter. Soon I was moving gingerly and self-assertively, carrying green salads with French mustard and olive oil to the table in wooden plates.

"This is my new major-domo, just being trained," Mr. Gernhardt introduced me to the guests.

I blushed.

"He's also an academic, a tennis player. Very versatile. He's gonna write the great American novel," said Mr. Gernhardt with a cheerful irony in his voice, while his guests glared at me as at an exotic fool, a chimpanzee, that's been let out of the zoo to run around free. It almost seemed as though the whole thing was a set-up, the main purpose of which was to ridicule me. Of course, I was aware that was a sensitive, self-centred, unrealistic sentiment I was having. Mr. Gernhardt licked a bit of wine from his glass, smacked his lips in a sour way, and raised his finger in a pontificating manner: "But whatever happens, watch out not to write about this, or I'll sue you for libel. Anyway, he keeps me good company when I come up here for the weekends, even plays decent chess."

I ground my teeth, but not very aggressively—not that I feared that I would look unfriendly. That goes without saying. I did. It did not extricate me from my decline into butlerhood, but merely confirmed it: a real servant is a grouchy servant. One of my molars felt unstable. I suspected that it had cracked, but I was not willing to find out, fearing the expenses. Dentistry is a serious problem if you've been raised in Eastern Europe and are living in the States. Since dentistry in Eastern and Central Europe is practically for free, it does not matter that we don't get the right minerals. It in no way interfered with low-budget, bohemian, lazybones lifestyles. But in the States, bad teeth are a financial disaster.

I lowered plates with meals from the right and left, forgetting the proper side from which to serve and clear up. The investment banker, the lawyer, and the doctor, who sat there with their wives or concubines, paid no attention to me whatsoever. I poured wine well and even devised a way of going from the kitchen to the dining room, which was adjacent, through a loop where nobody could see me; in such a way I drank a couple of glasses of wine myself. I snatched some crabmeat with that technique, but I didn't have enough time to chew it and swallowed it too soon, nearly choking, without the benefit of its taste.

The Chinese cook rushed me throughout the whole evening, and Mr. Gernhardt often cast impatient and discreet glances, when the guests were laughing and placing their palms onto each other's knees in the liberated genteel fashion, as if to punctuate a point of an anecdote. I had to bring an additional fork, or lift an empty plate in front of a radiant lady who ate only one fork-load from each dish. The cook looked terrified the whole evening.

While the guests licked desserts, I split wood with an axe in the backyard. I started a fire in the living room, and now and then stirred the coals, while the entourage discussed tax shelters, capital-gains laws, and the irrepressible yen. The fireplace looked like a mini-hell, I like a mini-devil, yet the clientele that belonged in hell sat safely away from the circle of fire. I stirred the embers with the fork-like spear, the embers broke, thinned, spitting sparks. My face felt warm, eyes blinded in the glowing orange redness, but just as I was beginning to soak up the heat, the cook tapped me alarmingly on the shoulder.

I had to rush to put ice in the silver trophy-like bowls, and place bottles of Champagne Brut in them. I harboured brutal thoughts while pouring champagne into the flimsy crystal glasses of my Caesaric industrialist and his fancy circle of friends or connections. I couldn't say exactly what they were.

A wife who was bored by discussions of finance asked from where my accent came, and I said "From myself," but that sounded rude, so I quickly corrected myself, and said, "Czechoslovakia."

She had been to Prague, and had some acute observations on it. "Oh, I love Prague! So lovely! Especially at night. There is no light there, so that the city looks like it must have in the last century during the Hapsburgs. In the moonlight, the buildings look so authentic. If you want to get a feel for the Habsburg elegance, you go to Prague!"

The company was rosy. I hauled more wood, collected the glasses, brought hot drinks in Chinese porcelain. Mr. Gernhardt talked about how labour was too expensive in America. That's why Japan used to have such an advantage over the West, and why Korea does. The solution was to have plants in Mexico, but that increased transportation problems. In fact, it was best to have foreigners work in the States. Amnesty for illegal aliens is no solution. Work permits with limited rights, so that the foreigners could gratefully concentrate on work and not on welfare.

At the end of the evening, I helped couples slide on their coats, escorted them through the appropriate doors into their respective cars, opening car doors for the ladies. The cook whisperingly taught me how to spread sheets over a guest bed, and then I did up the sheets in the master bedroom.

Loud knocks bumped me out of my sleep in the morning. The Chinese cook said I should cut more wood, set the fireplace, set the table for breakfast, and go shopping. He gave me a two-page shopping list.

While the guests strolled around the sunny pond, I vacuumed the carpets and the floor. Mr. Gernhardt occasionally dropped in since he mistrusted my industry, and in the spirit of giving me therapy, he told me to scrub the bathtubs and toilets in the four bathrooms. With my fingers bloating, I washed laundry with various club insignias, carried the luggage back and forth, and drove the dignified couple to the cinema twenty miles away, to watch *My Life as a Dog*. The woman applied a handkerchief to her eyes for half the trip home, and asked me not to cut the lanes in curves.

"It's safer that way," I said. "When you see a spot where the car can fit through, you better take it."

"No, it makes me nervous," she said, and next time I changed lanes I did it extremely slowly, so that I spent several minutes driving in the middle of the road, until a car honked. "See!" I said.

She leaned against Mr. Gernhardt as if in mortal danger.

After the trip, while the lady was taking a walk around the pond, Mr. Gernhardt gave me a stern lecture on how I should be considerate to his guests. In general, he said, the principle is "smooth." Smooth on the road, smooth at the table; no sudden jolts.

The music on the stereo was Vivaldi, Pachelbel, and some other unjolting masters.

It was a tremendous relief when the whole crew was gone. I bought a Led Zeppelin album and turned up the volume so loud that a speaker blew out.

After New Year's, Mr. Gernhardt called up, and said that the Christmas thing was such a roaring success, he and Ms. DuPont would come up again.

I had to clean up the place, set the bed sheets, so that no creases would show. I even tried to get the speaker repaired, thinking it was only a fuse, but no, it had croaked.

When they showed up, Mr. Gernhardt's eyes flashed into all the corners of the rooms, spotting spiderwebs and gentle collections of dust. "A disaster, disaster! The house is in an absolute mess." The cook gave me a lesson in proper cleaning techniques.

31

Mr. Gernhardt wanted his dose of Pachelbel, to soothe his nerves. "Oh, yes, I meant to tell you, I was listening to *Swan Lake*, and the thing just went silent. I don't know what happened."

"Probably just a fuse." He sent me to the audio store; I drove around the countryside and came back in half an hour with the grim news.

This time the lady no longer behaved like a guest. She was very much at home, ordering me around without using the time-consuming "please." She gazed through the windows. Deer floated in and out of the woods in waves, like dolphins, and fawns frolicked around the pond. She drew trees, carefully staring at them, as if it made any difference which way a branch curved.

I watered flowers and plants imported from the Brazilian jungles, mixing prescribed proportions of blue, green and yellow chemical nutrients into lukewarm water. The couple came up two weekends a month in the blue Mercedes, with mounds of flowers. Just a phase, I hoped. Next time they showed up, upon entering the retreat the lady said: "Oh, it's so lovely this time, so clean. Oh, Boris, you've done such a wonderful job." Mr. Gernhardt also congratulated me heartily, and the worst of it was that I felt good, flattered, proud, like a schoolboy who has done his homework. Of course, I caught myself in the middle of having these reactions, blushed. I was developing a servile personality with alarming rapidity and authenticity.

The lady loved flowers and she and I spent nearly an hour placing them in the appropriate Chinese vases. She began to chat in a friendly, relaxed manner. I guess she was used to confiding her contemplative thoughts to butlers. She advised me if I wanted to get to a woman's heart, I'd better give flowers. She shared some sentimental recollections of how good and graceful she was as a child to feel guilty while walking in her private zoo in Wilmington. I learned her husband had died in an air crash, in his private airplane in Alaska. Her son went to Princeton, and actually, he was just moving, so he needed some help. Could I help? Yes, of course.

I drove a pickup truck. I helped load the Persian carpets, stereo, wine crates of records and books, and the son, clearly taking after his mother, gingerly carried many delicate flowers in pots. I was treated to a meal at an undergraduate dining hall and nearly choked on roast beef, because God has punished me with appetites of all sorts, so that no matter what happens, I am tremendously hungry. I was not able to make much conversation with the boy.

"I don't know what exactly I'll do next summer," he declared, and it was clear that there was a moral dilemma behind the statement, and that the integrated youth with blue eyes would come through it morally triumphant.

"Well, if I were you, I'd go to the Himalayas," I said.

"No, the choice is between spending a summer at the Sorbonne studying French, and working in the hospital for the blind as a volunteer."

"What's there to think? It seems clear that the Sorbonne is the right choice, and as for the blind, you could pay somebody to do the volunteering for you."

"But it would be a good internship position. I want to go to medical school."

"No sweat, you'll get in."

"It's not that easy. Well, of course, I don't foresee any trouble there, but the point is not getting in, but gaining the experience. I want to be a good doctor."

"If you become a doctor, you'll get the experience eventually, I don't see how you could avoid it."

"You'd be surprised; many doctors are nearly incompetent. Haven't you read the article in *Time* magazine?"

"No ..."

"Don't you, as a writer, read a lot to keep up?"

"No, I am not a writer, and I'm even less of a reader."

To make the short story shorter, this gallant, good-hearted boy decided during the course of that very meal he would volunteer for the blind. As I gulped OJ, I stared at him through the bottom of the glass, genuinely perplexed; here we were, he a rich man rushing to work as much as possible, and I a penniless one living in leisure. I admired him, after all, for his gallant purposefulness, but I admired much more the paradox of him being work-stricken to my living in leisure.

"I hear it's a beautiful place where my mother and her friend spend time."

"Quite fine."

"She says she has a good time." He seemed to be probing to get the picture of what the hell his mom was doing with the toy manufacturer. And why shouldn't he know? I was, after all, eager to make a verbal picture of it all myself. I couldn't write about my weekend butlerhood to my friends, but with this boy, well, he knew what I was in; I could tell him, good heart and all that.

"Yes, not bad. The Chinese cook prepares brook trout, as well as sea spiders and other marine wonders for them, good stuff; I get to eat now and then the leftovers . . . real good; of course, they could buy fancier food, but they don't; they don't indulge in caviar; I don't know whether they have anything personally against it. Maybe because caviar is mostly Soviet and they don't want to support the evil empire."

I drove the furniture and all the stuff back to Bedford, and moved it into the storage room. Ms. DuPont thanked me heartily for helping her son . . . and seemed to like me and said, "Well, if you visit London, you could use our little apartment there, there's nobody using it—we're all too busy here—so when you have a vacation, you could go there. Or Paris, the same thing."

Next week, Mr. Gernhardt drove up alone. I stared around,

because I was so used to seeing Ms. DuPont, but she was not there, nor her little poodle—it was not leaping around or wagging its tail, with its little red tie like a walking Christmas present.

Mr. Gernhardt took me aside and on the steps, next to the peeping daffodils ready to sprout out of the ground, he asked me in a weepy voice, "You have been indiscreet?"

"Far be it from me, I am never indiscreet," I said.

"Just think about it."

I racked my brains and found no indiscretion that concerned him.

"What did you say to Ms. DuPont's son?"

"Nothing."

"Just think. Didn't you tell him anything of how we live here?"

"Nothing beyond what he asked me, and then far less . . ."

"Then you could have? How about: brook trout, sea spiders and other marine wonders?"

"Oh yes, brook trout. Well, you have those. They are not that expensive, and as for sea spiders and other marine wonders, well, that's a line from Gogol that I just couldn't help but insert there!"

"You have been indiscreet. Ms. DuPont and I live rather modestly here and everywhere, and she wants her son to think that. She wants to raise him in moderation, to be a good-hearted man. This is a great blow to her, and greater to me. You have no idea how dear a friend she is to me, and you have jeopardized our friendship. That's more than I can stand, and I am afraid our arrangement is terminated. I'm sorry it came to this, I've enjoyed your company here, but . . . anyway, it's all my fault, I should have known better than to have a writer stay here."

"But there's no harm done! I could tell the boy how cheap in fact the brook trout is, and he'll understand! I could show him my paycheque; he'll know that you aren't spending too much!"

That line seemed to incense him further. "I'm afraid you'll have to leave this afternoon. I cannot have you around anymore. Oh, god," he said, as if to himself, "I don't know whether she'll be back."

Of course, I realized how it must hurt to lose a multi-billion-aire friend. I walked dejectedly to my room, yet with a sense of re-lief, with no more of the abjection to which I had sunk on account of the downward pull of my cardinal weakness, namely, laziness.

I packed my things swiftly and soon was on the train to New York to visit my friends, to whom I retold anecdotally what had actually been taking place in Bedford. Now I could tell them be-cause I was no longer a part-time butler.

The prospect of looking for a job was gloomy, and I was very reluctant. What the hell could I do? Drive a cab? Word process? Naturally, I browsed through the Employment section of the *New York Times*, and nothing sounded good, except the computer sys-tem analysts with the $8,000 monthly starting salaries, but un-fortunately, that would take some more education. Health admin-istrators wanted, the career of the future, but again, not qualified. Truck drivers, well, I'd be sure to cause some accident with those huge monsters, sweep half the highway off a cliff in California. Cable TV sales for Westinghouse—well, that sounded good. I limped to the interview, the knuckles of my left foot hurting. Mr. Gernhardt had given me some black fancy shoes with Goodyear soles, the same firm that does the tires of Lotus Ford and some other Formula One cars, definitely very classy shoes. They were the right size but a little too narrow. I couldn't quite walk comfort-ably in Mr. Gernhardt's shoes, though I could look good in them, and that was all that mattered for the interview. What made me think that I would be a good salesman? I am friendly, outgoing, and I like to tell jokes and anecdotes. I fall into conversations with strangers wherever I go.

I was given the job. It turned out that it would be door-to-door in Harlem and the Bronx. So I continued reading the *New York Times*, and my eyes sort of naturally began to turn to the last pages, in which positions for domestics were advertised. I caught myself doing it, and shuddered with hurt dignity. Why, I was behaving like a professional butler!

Actually, the word butler was nowhere to be found in the ads; housekeeper, catering service, companion, domestic, au pair (for butleresses), and even house-sitter, which was the most deceptive euphemism. You have to pay a housekeeper a real salary, but if you give anything to your house-sitter, you are doing it out of the overflowing generosity of your heart, after which, the house-sitter shouldn't be brazen enough to refuse some "light" housekeeping interludes. In fact, the whole paper was filled with euphemisms that partly disguised the underlying bondage roles, the humiliations, since America is such an egalitarian society, or rather has the appearance of being one. I am sure that the rich bemoan the rhetorical extents to which they have to resort in order to obtain servants.

I looked through management positions. Perhaps I could be a manager? Experience, experience . . . unfortunately, a lazy man has no work experience. Then a step lower—management assistant, typing speed 55 a must—well, clearly, that's a euphemism for secretary. I threw the newspapers into the garbage. But wait a minute, how would I live? So I took the papers out of the garbage, with coffee grains all over them, and looked for social-work positions. There was one for fluent Russian speakers, to help Jewish refugees from the Soviet Union settle in Brooklyn. Of course, my Russian was atrocious, but perhaps they would not find out. I wrote an application and mailed it, and continued pacing up and down the apartment of my Indian friend, who was being entertained by watching me. He was a spot market trader, and told me that several days before he had lost ten grand because he had taken a shit at the wrong moment, just when the market was going haywire. When he had come out of the john, buckling up on the run, he saw the figures dropping; instantly he shrieked out and sold his stock, and the second he did that, the figures rebounded. Just as we both burst out in laughter about the financial anecdote, the phone rang. Mr. Gernhardt asked for me.

"I don't think we need to see each other," I said to him.

"Well, we could talk . . ."

The very same evening we were sitting at a Chinese restaurant; I was being treated. He said, "Ms. DuPont wants you back. She thinks that I overreacted. It's all okay between her and her son. She thinks you are going to be out in the streets and starving."

The last sentence sounded especially promising. I had hoped he would make out a cheque for five thousand dollars at least, for my psychological damages. Instead, he went on, "So we want you back! Will you come? I'll increase your pay to five hundred a month, and with a free car, free place, and only two weekends of work a month it's a deal you can't beat."

"Let me think about it."

"Actually, I was impressed with how you handled your being laid off without a scene, stoically. So I would like to have you back as well."

The whole thing must have started with the son.

I said, "All right, it might not be too bad."

"Incidentally, I checked out the prices. Bluefish, your staple, is more expensive than brook trout. Have you noticed that?" He said it in the voice of an unjustly accused party.

Ms. DuPont, Mr. Gernhardt, the cook and I drove out into the country. The trees were budding, the sun throwing a sparkling gloss over ponds, windows, and cars; the country looked exceptionally redolent. This time Mr. Gernhardt was going for a three-week vacation to the Fiji Islands so, if nothing else, I could have three weeks with a nice place to stay and no work.

But things were not that simple in the spring. As soon as I got my things back into my old room, Mr. Gernhardt took me into the garden, and asked me to scrape out all the leaves that were stuck in thorny bushes, to pick up branches on the edge of the woods and to stack them in piles, to plant dozens of varieties of flowers, and so on. So, in other words, I would now be a resident gardener.

For the three weeks it was fine, but when Mr. Gernhardt returned from his vacation, he complained that the garden was ruined, so now we worked in it together. The flowers were absolutely essential for keeping his woman friend around, so each broken flower was deplorable. Cutting grass with bunches of daffodils and rocks in it was very complicated, because the broad lawnmower kept getting stranded over rocks, the blade hitting them so that sparks flew.

Because deer chewed flower petals, I was supposed to erect a fence around many of the bunches. I hammered spikes into the ground with a sledgehammer, but the ground was so rocky that it was extremely difficult to put up the fences. I developed tennis elbow in the process, and Ms. DuPont and her buddy complimented me. In the evening, as I served them Chinese tea, I overheard their conversation; she was wondering to which museum to bequeath a collection of British landscape paintings and to which one to give money outright for expanding a Chinese painting section. Why couldn't she give me some money, not much, just enough so I wouldn't have to put up with the humiliations of part-time butlerhood? Unfortunately, how could I tell her that? I ran to my room and brought back my copies of Michelangelo drawings, several self-portraits, drawn out of vanity when I had a goatee (that made me look like a junior Mr. Gernhardt, a leaner, darker, and more glaring version). In my humility, I complained that I would like more subjects.

"These are wonderful!" exclaimed Ms. DuPont. "I'd like to commission you to make a large charcoal portrait of Mr. Gernhardt!"

Joy crept through my body, but Mr. Gernhardt said, "Wonderful, oh, no, dear, let me handle that. I'll commission you!" and he looked at me so inimically that I understood that commissioning meant something quite different, like "piss off!"

I went back to my room, swearing. I knew the penny-pincher wouldn't bother to pay me for a drawing, and he didn't want her to pay me, because indirectly it would be like her paying me. He had bigger plans for her. Still, I eavesdropped a little as they were mentioning figures, because large figures have a charming sound to my ears, and I thought, shit, at least this is real life, I am in contact with real life. They were getting stuck in calculation, and Mr. Gernhardt exclaimed, "I'll give it to my mathematician. He ought to be able to solve that." Incidentally, he liked to label people as his: *my cook, my mathematician, my computer wiz, my designer, my driver, my electrician, my chemical engineer*, and no doubt, when he was outside of my earshot, he called me *my country butler*.

During the summer solstice, Mr. Gernhardt hosted another lobster brunch. An investment banker, a buddy of his dressed in brick colours, was sitting outdoors with his red-haired son, a Harvard college kid; his redhead wife, an interior designer; and the son's kinky-redhaired girlfriend. The Chinese cook prepared brunch, brought out the first course, and then had to leave for his son's graduation. I had told Mr. Gernhardt I would not bother with breakfasts and lunches, because alongside the garden they were threatening to increase my workload unpleasantly close to full time. Actually, I had explained to him that I would do no flower planting or transplanting either. So, in the background of the crew's lunch on the patio, you could see a professional gardener bending over near the pond, sticking baby flowers into the ground, so that it looked like Mr. Gernhardt had not only a cook and a butler, but a gardener as well. As I was reading *Molloy Dies*, my wonderful benefactor kept calling my name. "Could you please bring out the salad?" .... "Could you please clear the lunch plates and bring out the dessert plates?" .... "Could you ..."

After each of these, I snapped at him, "Do you think that I am your butler or something? I am a house-sitter. You bring it out for yourself."

The investment banker looked at me with an air of being scandalized. The Harvard brat looked at me with wide learning eyes, analyzing perhaps the psychology of a butler, and the girlfriend barely suppressed her giggles, looking sideways at the bushes. Mr. Gernhardt seemed to be suppressing rage, but he said nothing. With an air of hurt dignity, he served coffee, with the assistance of the smooth son, while I put on a Liszt piano concerto in my room, loud, so I would not have to listen to the odious clanking of china and New York and Boston accents. Not that I have anything against New York and Boston, but at the moment I did.

I expected Mr. Gernhardt would dismiss me from the job, and I was looking forward to exchanging insults with him. He resisted, perhaps thinking it was just a phase, a butler's crankiness, which should be smoothed over by an increase in salary. Namely, he had taken it that I had gone on a temporary strike, in the manner of Polish and Czech workers.

Now he didn't make many demands, except that I had to adjust the pool pH factor, which I didn't mind since I was the one who used it more than anybody else. I had guests who sunbathed, in one instance a whole family. The daughter of the family did not let her father get into the water naked, and she rebuked him when he smoked pot. A friend often dropped off his wife to sunbathe there while he went to work. The wife was attractive and flirtatious ("Mark, how come all your male friends are so handsome?" she said when she met me, so that, shameless as I was, I nearly blushed). At a party she asked me to give her a backrub in front of her husband, and when I refused, she insisted that I do it, since I had said that I gave the best backrubs in the county. When I finally gave her the backrub she moaned, saying she had not felt so good in years, that it beat lovemaking. She followed me wherever I went, like a duckling following its mother. She wanted to set me up with her girlfriends, and was always most enthusiastic in my company. When she was left alone at the pool, I had a sensation of erotic tension; especially so when the three of us were in the water. I was proud of myself that I had resisted her, which I confided to the husband over several bottles of wine in a SoHo winery. He must have told her about it, because next time I saw them, she crankily declared that what I called a "data-entry operator" meant nothing but a "secretary," and she puffed air out of her nostrils snortingly, like a lean, graceful racehorse passing by a mule early in the morning. It seemed to me that she would have resented me less if we had committed adultery. That was the risk of being open: losing a friend. Their story was a classic of sorts. He had had hardly any money, and she came from a fairly well-to-do family. He'd put on a show of being rich, bought a fancy car on credit, invested all his money in courting her and, getting the impression that he was rich, she fell for him. The disappointing revelation came, as it could not be hidden; she was nearly disowned by her family. But the husband worked zealously as a computer salesman, and began to make pots of money, whereupon the family recognized him as a decent member. The two of them put up a ritzy show wherever they went, and they liked my new house-sitting location, speculating how much the country house cost, and how many years it would take them to get a place like that.

At any rate, one weekend Mr. Gernhardt and Ms. DuPont were sunbathing, and I was told to put in more chemicals, to kill the bacteria. "The water is so green!" said the toy manufacturer.

"What do you want it to be, pink? Grass and leaves fall in, the green is reflected from the trees. Of course it's green."

"No, it comes from the bacteria. You haven't done your job, you haven't put enough chemicals in the water, have you?"

Just then a little frog leaped out of the water, and Ms. Dupont screamed.

"Why, there are more than enough chemicals. You want to poison yourself? See, the water used to be healthy enough for frogs to jump in, and now the poor dear is rushing for its life," I said with the tremor of compassion on my vocal cords.

Ms. DuPont looked up at me with slanting eyes.

"Yes, put in more chemicals," said Mr. Gernhardt.

"That's no way to go," I said, staring at Mrs. Chemistry herself. "To kill off everything natural. You think that's healthy?"

Neither of them spoke, but looked at me as if I were a member of the Green party, or rather of some other party, a Nazi party, though of course, that would have been preferable for the chemistry wealth hoarder, whose family had grown rich selling gun powder in the First World War to whomever would buy it, to both sides, so that there never was any shortage of means to murder. Actually, even Mr. Gernhardt's toys are made of compound plastics. When these thoughts all caught up with me, I chuckled, and poured in more chemicals than I was asked to. Ms. Dupont looked at me a couple of times contemptuously, and rubbed more lotion on her forehead, corrected the position of the sliced cucumbers beneath her eyes, and turned her head towards the sun. Soon several silvery swollen frog bellies surfaced and floated on the water. The two manufacturers lay without noticing the bellies, their own bellies receiving the benevolence of the sun expansively. When they were about to enter the water, they shuddered at the sight of the frogs, and in disgust quickly left the scene, glancing at me sideways, as if the next thing I would do would be to make them float like that.

Mr. Gernhardt left again for three weeks. The professional grass-cutters, as well as the gardener, covered only a limited area. I let the grass grow and the deer break through fences to eat fragile flowers from exotic climates, artificial and vulnerable transplants anyway. I didn't resurrect the fences. I didn't sweep all the floors.

One Friday afternoon Mr. Gernhardt showed up, accompanied by a young man who exuded unfeigned servility—clearly he had been broken in at another estate and probably held a temporary visa.

"Let me introduce you," said Mr. Gernhardt theatrically, enjoying the scene. "This is Roberto, my new house-sitter. I expect you to vacate the premises by five o'clock." Then he looked around, his face contorting in shock at the sight of his garden. Roberto tried to talk to me politely in the meantime, in a thoroughly atrocious English. It's hard to be polite in bad English. You want? You like?

My Indian friend Rama-Krishna laughed at me for lasting so long there and began to persuade me to get down on the floor as a trader, and to join the pack of screaming money grabbers in the pit. Instead, I wanted to work as a car salesman, but having been rejected on account of not having experience, I applied for a "sky is the limit" job; a fancy sales job that, in reality, turned out to be selling fire extinguishers. I was covering the Garment District. The technique: you walk in, pour gasoline over your leather bag, set it on fire with a lighter, and employ the extinguisher. A beam of vapours hisses, and the fire collapses with a thump, a sound of implosion. You sneeze from the gas. The fire is no more, and there's no sign on the leather of there ever having been a fire. In the meantime, the Hassidic furrier is pressing his palm against his chest, wondering whether he's having a heart attack, and you say, "See! Marvellously effective! Liquid gas!" And the furrier screams, "Get out!" I had even less luck working the car dealerships; at a gaseous BMW dealership in Chelsea I was thrown out by two large German-accented managers, while the supervisor screamed, "This whole place could have exploded!"

"That's why you need the fire extinguisher!" I screamed from the door. "Better living with chemistry!"

But I must have offended the gods of chemistry; in three weeks of sales I sold not a single liquid-gas extinguisher (I worked on commission), and I got bronchitis from the chemicals irritating my bronchi. I ended up as a word-processing bum at Paine Webber, with charts and sheets of large figures pouring onto me from all sides, from young, haughty "analysts," work mules on their way up, throwing loads onto the donkeys on their way down/up, nowhere. Although I must say, I experienced a sort of prophetic future there: one of the first emails in the world with an attachment, in 1982, emailed to Houston. A Scottish man and I fumbled around with a manual to learn how to send the email, and called to confirm it had gone through. And it had.

Strings

On Columbus and 106th, opposite a hotel whose yellow sign bore a green monkey hanging by its tail, near a burnt-down cancer ward, I shared an apartment with three Juilliard students. At first, there were five of us: my ex-Soviet roommate's brother was there. The two ex-Soviets, fresh from an exile camp in Vienna, spoke no English and didn't dare leave the apartment. They spent the whole summer on a floor mattress, wrapped in a white sheet, gazing at a small TV we had found in a garbage heap on the Upper East Side. The antenna could catch only one trembling channel, which shifted up and down. When the summer was over, the ex-Soviets finally stood up from the bed, able to speak fluent English. The brother moved out and opened an ESP therapeutic centre in Chinatown.

A French violinist slept on the floor in an Alpine sleeping bag. Whenever he woke up, he rubbed his sweaty and hairy chest with a thick towel, and his bloodshot eyes stared at us as though we were Andean cannibals, cooking him for supper. As we had no air conditioning, on hot days he woke up in puddles of his own sweat.

I slept on a carpet from a rich man's garbage heap. The only one of us who had a real bed was the Swiss cellist, who shaved twice a day and resentfully looked around him at the chaos the rest of us created from our clothes, papers, bread crumbs, utensils, shoe-shine boxes, and vinyl records. I got used to the bohemian atmosphere, and paid no thought to how different it all was from what I had first expected of my time in America.

But as my roommates and I ran after a rat through our apartment, stumbling over ashtrays, beer cans, unwashed plates with dry egg yolks, it occurred to me: is this any way to live?

I didn't wish to chase the rodent; he looked like a veteran of many battles, and that he was in the predicament of having a crew of Juilliard musicians after him was no doubt a result of his observing us for a while, and correctly assessing us to be a bunch of wimps, whining day in and day out. He used to enter the kitchen at noon, charge the trash bag like a small boar, biting straight through the olive plastic for cheese crusts. We bought gourmet cheeses—since we didn't snort coke, we had to have some wasteful vice—which tasted the way cow dung, horse shit, and freshly cut grass smelled; strange how you grow to like a foul taste, the fouler, the tastier. The Frenchman scoffed at us for liking bland cheeses. The stench of cheese must have taken our rat back to his rural roots.

In the rat's first appearances, it was enough to set your foot in the kitchen, and he'd scurry off, squealing for life. But after he had heard us playing Schubert string quartets, his caution disappeared. Now he rummaged through our garbage languidly, looking fat and well-established. With an air of dignity, he strolled into the living room for the afternoon intermezzo.

Schubert moved him. I read somewhere that Bach moves plants. Schubert rooted our rat to the spot, making him tremble to the harmonics of minor keys, raising his hairs, so that he resembled a hedgehog. Now and then he stood on his hind legs, and put his paws together like a squirrel praying for a pistachio. Perhaps he would have clapped his paws, but didn't dare out of piety for the music.

Der Tod und das Mädchen was his absolute favourite. We used to play it sometimes just to tease him. Then he'd come quite close to the cello, his little beady eyes shone with tears, his upper lips twitched, and with his little incisors he pinched his lower lip. If his ears hadn't been so small, his tail so thin and wet, he could have passed for a squirrel and would have been quite likable. But Lord knows, he was not likable. Perhaps he wished to be. Perhaps he wished to make friends with us, and would have been proud of us. Perhaps he was proud of us. He may have even loved us. But we didn't appreciate him as the audience—after all, playing to entertain a rat is not what you'd call a lustrous career. Yet his listening always humoured us and instilled a *joie de vivre*, otherwise so hard to come by, into our strings.

But we had to put a stop to his increasing brazenness. Soon he would have been jumping on the table and dining with us. He would have grown so attached to us that he would have followed us on our dates. And, certainly, he would have been unstoppable if he had known Schubert's *Unfinished Symphony* would caress the walls at Avery Fisher Hall, though I should think he'd have preferred it at Carnegie Hall, where walls, old and sandy, must be easier to bite through.

We discovered that he feared Bartok. I don't know why he feared Bartok; maybe he hadn't been educated well enough to take the stresses of modernity in music, though he must have kept up with other modernities and postmodernities as a New York City rat. Though Bartok made him run for shelter, we couldn't keep playing Bartok just to keep a rat away.

Alone, none of us could have handled the little devil. But united—a Frenchman, a Yugoslav, an ex-Soviet, and a Swiss—we dared to attack him. Actually, the Frenchman was away on a date with a woman from the fourth floor. He had preferred a woman from the second floor, but one floor of elevator time was not enough for him to let her pick him up—that's how he described it. Three floors of elevator time sufficed for a woman to pick him up. So, the three of us intervened.

As the rat strolled into our bathroom, we exchanged looks. It was too much; now he wanted to share our toilet! The ex-Soviet jumped and shut the bathroom door, swearing in Russian. The Swiss and I grabbed the table, the plates sliding and crashing on the floor. We barred the bathroom door with the tabletop against it. Then we pulled the table back and aimed blows at him with a broomstick, a baseball bat (with which we had tried to Americanize ourselves), and one of the unscrewed table legs. Only two of us could fit in the doorframe at a time, so we took turns. Mostly we missed. The Swiss struck him first with the broomstick. The blow surprised the rat and incensed him. He shrieked gorily and jumped toward us. I got goosebumps from the shrillness of his voice. We were almost ready to beat a retreat, but we were too ashamed to give up.

The rat jumped again, right up to the edge of the table. As he was falling down, I struck him with the baseball bat, which brushed his back and squashed his tail on a tile. The tile broke in half. Hardly a second later, the table leg struck him, blowing him off the floor; his body hit the heating pipe. Now he jumped without any order, like a panicky frog, in such high leaps that he could have jumped over our barrier. He jumped left, and right, and then backward. He fell into the bathtub. He leaped but couldn't jump out of the slippery tub. We flung the table aside, the Swiss squealed "Ya'ohl," and we all jumped forward. From the side of the tub we aimed blows at the rat. Blood squirted. The enamel of the tub cracked in many places, revealing raw iron.

When he was finally dead, instead of feeling triumphant, we were ashamed. Slowly we swept his remains onto a Sunday *New York Times Magazine* and put it all into three olive garbage bags. In a sombre, funereal mood, we threw the bags into a rusty garbage bin. We washed the tub for days with all sorts of soaps. We threw away the clubs; henceforth, our table had only three legs. None of us took baths anymore, only showers, which changed from hot to cold to hot of their own accord.

If we had hoped that after the assassination we would be rat-free, we were wrong. A chap similar to our murdered friend began to appear, so similar that it spooked us. But he didn't care for music. We bought rat poison and put it in cheese. Either it didn't kill him or another rat indistinguishable from him replaced him. At night there were constant noises coming from the walls: scuffling of rats in their love, work (tunnel and road construction), and debates in muffled squeals.

One night a fire alarm went off. We didn't bother to get out of our beds; the alarm went off so often that it always seemed a prank. But when hollering reached our ears and smoke our nostrils, we looked out the window. Blue and orange tongues of fire licked the walls. We grabbed our passports, diplomas, money and instruments, and left behind pictures of families and girlfriends, suits, records, music scores. In long underwear we ran down the smoky stairways out of the building, into the slushy snow. Rats leaped out the windows, thumping against the pavement and then scurrying away.

Waiting for shelter, I got such frostbite in my large toe that for a while it seemed it would have to be cut off, and probably would have been if I'd had a good enough insurance policy to visit a doctor. I still can't feel anything in the toe. An orange school bus took us to shelter, and some shelter it was! People sick beyond repair, derelicts, drunks, drug addicts, lunatics, failed thieves who were still trying. We ran out of the stench for our lives and spent the night all rolled up in a bundle on a subway grate, in a stream of urinated heat.

Several days later, the Frenchman, the ex-Soviet and I moved back into our apartment. The Swiss cellist moved back to Switzerland. Although the building was now all sooty with the windows gaping black, our part was nearly intact. There were no rats there, not for a year, when we filed a claim against our landlord in small-claims court, demanding to be paid back several months of rent because there had been no hot water and heat. Although the land-lord didn't show up in court, he won the case and evicted us.

My Hairs Stood Up

We could live more easily in the country, but we like to be where the excitement is. We have always wanted to be around humans, to be as close to them as possible, to be their pets.

We have failed. Humans prefer animals neither as bright nor as capable as us, with the exception of a few unfixed cats. They keep all imaginable sorts of worms, monkeys, snakes, and marine monsters and still would not have us. Oh, to be sure, some humans keep some variety of our species, guinea pigs. But guinea pigs are nothing more than an inferior breed of us, and they are treated well by humans because humans are fond of inferiority in others.

I have always admired humans. What intelligence, what perseverance, what industry! I mean, they are doing more these days than we are. I cannot keep up with their technology anymore. I used to be able to enjoy their greasy cogs—if you got hungry, you could always get by around oily machines. Now, their machines are greaseless, cold inedible boxes.

Nowadays, even such a simple thing as a snack is dangerous; much of the food that seems to have been casually left over is poison for us. When tired of cement, you used to be able to take a stroll in the park. Now, you must abstain from eating, and what kind of fun is it to spend a sunny day in the park, starving? The streets are even worse: as soon as you are in the open, humans step on you, throw stones, iron, whatever happens to be in their front paws. They are mean. Where did they get this urge to kill? Not even cats are like that; they don't bother us. Actually, we are too tough for them. Nor do they bother mice, unless famished or for play; only young cats hunt mice in the frivolity of their youth. But humans will kill and kill and it's never enough for them. They do it neither to feed themselves, nor to enjoy themselves. Killing actually disgusts them, and yet somehow that's why they want to kill all the more, by any means they can imagine. They take pride in the ingenuity with which they can kill us. They set up traps for us. The chemicals in the traps are more poisonous by the day. They get cats—and put up with their most obnoxious smells—to kill us. They hate us. I don't know how else to explain it.

They think we are ugly, and yet they keep bulldogs, who resemble us but are neither as good-looking nor as smart as us.

Speaking of similarities, I have concluded that humans are similar to us. Humans believe the same thing. Whenever they have questions about themselves, they seek answers with us. If they have a problem regarding their intelligence, they test us. If their livers hurt, they test our livers. If their eyes go blind, they test our eyes even before they will test their own. The assumption, a correct one, is that if something is harmful to us, it is harmful to them, and that if we don't understand something, they don't either. We are siblings, we and humans. They live in walls, so do we. They eat old, burnt food, any kind of rotten food actually; they even intentionally rot foods in greasy water. I don't see any essential dissimilarities between us, except that humans are bigger and, therefore, live in bigger holes in walls. Their world is merely our world magnified. And yet, instead of friendship, which we had sought for so long, they feel animosity towards us. We must hide from them, and they need not hide from us, even though they fear us. I am not exaggerating when I say that their lives are an antithesis to ours—because of their gross misunderstanding of us. If they cooperated with us, provided us with clean conditions, we would carry no diseases for them, and we would create miracles in science together. Of course, now that we are pushed and shoved underground, we run into many health hazards, but most of the diseases that we contract come from the humans to us, not the other way around.

They make their new buildings mostly with us in mind—hermetically sealed. I've had some adventures trying to enter one of those new buildings of theirs. You often have to go through sewage, which is risky business because the shit may just pour all over you. But you grin and bear it and let yourself be washed into a broader pipe where you can catch a breath and have another go. To avoid the avalanche, you never go up during the day or evening.

Once the water shot me up a vertical branch; I took the first horizontal turn, and reached a narrower pipe. I thought there would never be an end to it, and my lungs were about to burst, when I was finally shot out of the water. There was poison packed in grated plastic, which gave me enough of a footing to jump out. I slid on the porcelain floor. I rushed to hide behind a smelly metal box which growled and even crunched ice. I tried to climb into the box, lured by the smells of dead fowl. The box was too tall for me, and I was curious about other large cubicles. Clearly, it was one of those modern buildings where it's hard to bite your way through. I prefer the old ones of cement and wood. Biting through wood is very good for you: it keeps your jaws strong, sharpens your teeth, relaxes you, and cheers you up in teamwork. We take turns on a project of occupying a building, making networks of holes as corridors. Wood spurs you on into artistic playfulness. Having criss-crossed hundreds of old buildings, however, I found this new one, though less to my liking, tremendously mysterious. Still, in a large space, the first thing I rushed to was a large old crate, stretching to the ceiling along a whole wall. The crate was filled with thin vertical papers bound by thick paper and cloth. I took a brief snooze, my 21st nap. I nap a lot and count time accordingly. Sunlight woke me up through a crack. I was surprised that the new building, supposed to be nearly hermetically sealed, would have wooden boxes with cracks, but I've heard that humans grow sentimental and wish, as they go into the future, to be able to go into the past at the same time—that's greed for you. So they get all kinds of boxes from dead humans, who got the boxes from other dead humans, and the more generations a thing has lasted, the crazier humans are about it.

I peeked out of my crack. Several humans of varying sizes sat at a horizontal plank of wood on four sticks, and walked between the elevated plank of wood and a big white box where they keep winter. They cracked and sucked some eggs they had stolen from chickens, drank black steaming water from burnt beans, squealed and growled a bit, and then walked out of the cubic space.

I took a couple of bites from the bound paper just to play down my hunger. Maybe you could live on that paper; there must be something nutritious about it: probably those dark things in boring shapes, running one after another in lines, looking like the droppings of flies. The lead-smelling shapes however are squeezed into squares—a mark that humans have arranged them. I like the taste of leaded cellulose though I am not exuberantly fond of paper.

Having grown certain nobody was in the large cubic hole, I crept out for a stroll. I didn't feel quite safe, as if something might hit me from behind, so I did my walking against the walls quickly, and actually, it must have looked more like running. Well, I admit it, I was kind of running.

I crawled into a white box, where they keep summer with the sun in zenith. Actually, it can be so hot in those boxes that I think they keep hell there. I crawled in through a hole against the wall, climbed through a narrow passage and to another hole into the centre cubicle, the baking chamber. It still smelled of various animals that had been broiled for human pleasure. It raises the hair on my tail to think how humans put innocent creatures into the gas chambers to burn them! After my tour through the hell-box, I returned to the lead-paper and took an intoxicating snooze.

A noise of humans woke me up. Through the crack, I saw one human opening the hell-box and another sliding into it a metal board with a large animal carcass on it. I couldn't tell at first what animal it was—it had only two legs, without feet, sticking up, and it had no fur or feathers, and was much too large to be a chicken. At first I thought it could be an infant human. They gazed languidly at the carcass in the hell-box. And then again, nothing, except smells of burning flesh. I spent a lot of time sniffing the lead on the paper, snoozing more than normal, and not daring to leave the crate. Later on, humans gathered around the elevated plank and squatted on smaller planks of wood around it. With their front paws, they held up thin transparent stones filled with liquid, knocking them against each other and gazing longingly at each other, then gulped the pale liquid cautiously. I guess it may have been their urine, though it smelled like grapes. Then they ate some grass. After a while of that, one of them opened the hell-box. The smell of burning flesh ignited my adventurous bone. They pulled the flesh out of the hell-box and let it sit on top, then went into another cubic space.

I was not brave enough to leave my shelter right away. But soon I sensed they would be gone for a while and I crept out of my shelter and climbed up to the flesh container. I worked my way through the heat into its centre. Oh, Dracula, how hot it was there! I sneaked into the animal to protect myself from the heat. The inside of the animal was large and spacious—I could have easily lived in it with a whole family, despite there being some muddy wheat. What better than to have living space with edible walls! Soon I was so groggy that I couldn't move.

Only vaguely did I hear the people return. I was presently being rocked left and right and lifted up, judging by my suddenly seeming heavier. I surmised that the board and the animal were being placed on the elevated plank of wood. The walls of the tur-key—I had noticed atrophied wings on the side of the body and I had concluded it must be a turkey—shook and I heard a dull sound. When streaks of light penetrated into my chamber, I real-ized that the humans were tearing the flesh off the turkey with their long iron claws. They keep plenty of such removable claws around food because their natural ones are no good. On one side, they reached the ribs. The tearing stopped. In trepidation I won-dered whether they could see me as I could see them. I decided that from light one cannot see well into darkness, but from darkness one can see into light only too well. Through a narrow space be-tween two thin ribs in a crack on flimsy stomach lining I saw one human, refracted and distorted. It was cutting streaks of light flesh and streaks of dark flesh, piercing it with metal claws, and lifting it into its mouth. The human shouted. I cannot tell the moods of humans from their faces. I don't think they have moods and emotions. I know they scream and squeal and grunt and hiss, and mostly, they rattle quite monotonously. It is a strange custom they have, to gurgle noise when they are more than one. Maybe they keep themselves at bay from each other by their constant noise, the way dogs keep away from each other by growling and cats by spitting. Well, if my supposition that they hate one another (in a cold, unemotional way) is true, then I don't understand why they gather in groups so often. And if they are alone, they have special boxes that rattle out similar noises, flickering all kinds of lights and some only shades of grey. After making sounds with its throat, the human was quiet. It stretched its lips and showed its flat teeth. I don't know what they have teeth for, when they cut their food with artificial claws, and they cut walls with big metal claws.

It was pleasantly warm, and I could begin to breathe without strain. I did not dare move enough to eat the flesh around me. All of a sudden, the human stood up and light flashed into my eyes from a large metal surface. The metal cut into the bird and more light poured into my shelter. I knew there was no more time to hesitate. Lest I should be cut with the edge of the super-claw, I jumped out of the bird. I staggered, weakened by having been in heat for so long, blinded by light. But I didn't stay still. I jumped forward, for you mustn't stay still when humans are around, although they are very slow. You must never underestimate these slow-moving and intelligent creatures. I often think it is a miracle how it is possible for creatures that think and react so slowly to build complex machines. I am not quite sure that it is really these humans who build, for example, houses. Well, to make a long story short, I leaped out of the bird. I landed in a warm container of squashed cranberries. I slid trying to jump out of it. There were many high-pitched sounds in the room. My heart skipped beats, but when it did beat, it made up for the missed ones; it beat frantically. I jumped over and over again. The white stone container of squashed cranberries tipped over; I ran, jumped over the edge of the elevated plank of wood. I fell into the lap of a human with bare legs. Some humans wrap their legs and others leave their legs bare. The things they use for wrapping are soft and fun to chew; I heard they were squashed balls of cotton. Actually, I had never chewed their wrappings, and now I had no time to take up that experience as, at any rate, there was enough new experience pouring into my life, and I wanted to make sure that experience would not be in the form of blows. I bounced off the lap, which was changing angles as the human was falling onto the floor. The chair squeaked and the human screamed. But I have already said there was a lot of screaming. I am repeating myself. Never mind. They were repeating themselves too. I did not know why they screamed so much. I sort of wished to think that it was all because of me. But I was too humble to dare to imagine that those powerful creatures that raised inedible buildings would have given little me so much recognition. When I thought of it tears of pride began to flow down the fur of my cheeks. Well, they would have flowed if I hadn't shivered at the thought that a detachable human hind paw of compressed ox-hide might be flying at me. Someone else fell on the floor—it was a furry floor but I couldn't figure out what sort of animal they had skinned for the fur—with a dull thud and a piercing shriek. Some people were falling on the floor, while others remained standing. A couple of humans were throwing their metal claws at me. I ran behind a white box. I recalled that I should never judge humans on the basis of their awkwardness. They are awkward and slow, but suddenly, Puff, Gotcha! Well, these humans were preoccupied enough. Some stood up, others squatted, and they ate no more. On the contrary, some vomited right there on the floor, others over the elevated plank of wood and over the turkey. Then they took everything that was on the table and put it into dark plastic bags. What a pity that the half-digested food all went to waste. But I was not in the mood to save the food by storing as much of it as possible in my stomach. First I wanted to save my stomach. I enjoyed seeing them walk out of the room in their usual vulnerable manner, on hind legs—when I used to love them, I worried they might trip any moment. Once they were gone, I scurried across the floor and I slipped into a garbage bag, where I found the bird. I hid inside its walls once again; that was the only way I could think of escaping, knowing they would throw it out sooner or later.

I have just said, ". . . when I used to love them." Do I no longer love them? That's right. They are arrogant dirty bastards. Yet we have courage to eat what they eat, and to sniff what they sniff. On the other paw, they would not touch what we eat. That's not fair. I loathe humans. I spent so much time liking them. I could not just like and like without encouragement to go on. I hate them. I mean, the way they cut up some of us, the weakest among us, in their experiments, and feed us poisons to see just how we'd take it, that is wicked. And how many times have they nearly killed me?

Now, I could have killed some of their old ones, but I haven't done it yet. Whenever I entered their cubicles and sniffed the air, I could tell whether there were old feeble mammals there still breathing. I could have easily chewed their necks and bit through their jugulars; I was considerate and let them sleep on. It is true, though, that whenever I ran into some who didn't breathe, I began to tear their flesh, making the point that they were animals clean enough to eat. But look at how they treat us: they tear us apart while we are still alive, and when we are dead, they throw away our corpses without ever considering them edible, even though our flesh is more nutritious and richer in minerals than theirs.

Humans have repaid our kindness with hatred, our admiration with contempt, our service of cleaning the mess after them, with poisoning us; our love with murder. They are resilient to all kinds of poisons because half of their diet is poison, and they constantly introduce new poisons just for the taste of it. But we will outlast them.

Tumbling: Daruvar

I remember a wedding my cousin, who is eight years older than me, had in Daruvar. He was the first rock musician in town, a lead guitarist with flared jeans, an irrepressible smile, long curly black hair, and cowboy boots with exceedingly high heels—he was short. I don't remember the bride. On a record, Ike and Tina Turner sang, *In the year 2525, if man is still alive, if a woman can survive* . . . I was fourteen. A lot had already happened. Jimi Hendrix had died, and shortly after him, Jim Morrison. My father had died before them both. My world was shattered, and now strangely it had opened up with this blinding beam of sunlight. Cousin Mrvica— Crumb, we called him—was getting married. The concept of weddings felt off in that moment. I sat off on my own, resentful that people wanted me to drink and dance. I would do neither. I observed the dancing around me and only thought, *Why are Jimi and Jim and father dead?* Their music was more provocative. Or maybe it wasn't. On the record, Ike and Tina had grown apocalyptic. By the year 7510, *I guess it's time for Judgment Day.* The song sent a shiver of doom across my skin, into my narrow Italian shoes. My balding and flushed uncle was fiddling with a guitar and sweat sparkled off his forehead. His blind wife smiled, revealing her gold tooth as she swayed to the rhythm. My cousin, who had married a Hungarian welterweight boxing finalist from Argentina named Sonyi—who was no longer welterweight—danced and drank and laughed too. I had no idea that only Mrvica, Sonyi, and me would be alive a few decades later. My cousin Nina died in excruciating pain from lupus a few years after the wedding. Mrvica lives alone. Most of the party was felled by horrific misfortune. I sat there, gloomy as a night forest in November without leaves and snow. Very few of my other cousins were there, although we were a family with many cousins—I had 30 of them. Drago, my red-faced uncle, a fine singer who very soon afterward would die of a massive heart attack, slipped me a glass of wine and winked. The wine was sweet, terribly sweet, like a kosher wine. I drank the glass, and felt all the worse for it, and decided I wouldn't make such a mistake again. I wondered why wine was such a standard feature at weddings, why Jesus turned wine into water for a wedding. Did he drink at the wedding, and how much? It seemed at Mrvica's wedding, the wine disappeared, and people drank Seltzer water in the end. *I am glad, I am glad, I am glad*, sang Cream. So this is it, this is the joy that awaits you, miserable weddings and Communist Party meetings, I thought, conversing with my alienated self, and thought, get me out of here. And guess what, I am not out of here, and I am sort of glad for it—actually very glad.

Byeli: The Definitive Biography of a Nebraskan Tomcat

Making the decision not to castrate Byeli did not go smoothly. At the Fine Arts Work Center in Provincetown, some idle poets declared that my wife and I belonged to the Mormon sect because we wouldn't castrate our cat. The poets deplored our decision as most monstrous because the tomcat would suffer cuts, torn ears, bruises, and he would make many female cats suffer and give birth to too many cats, who would give birth to more, which would cause an infinite amount of suffering, directly to befall our irresponsible selves.

Byeli was an orphan. In the shrubs of the periphery of Austin, Texas, a ten-year-old boy found him, all furry skin and ribs, about five weeks old. Jeanette adopted the kitten, and because it was white, she and her French roommate named it Neige, snow.

Before I heard of Neige, I dreamed I was trying to kick away a white cat with three sickly limbs, away from my teepee.

While Jeanette banged the door on her pickup, having just arrived to join me on the Cape, the little tom strutted into the apartment. I renamed him Snyeshko, "snowman" in Croatian.

At two months he roamed as much as three hundred yards and tailgated a homeless female. She often flared up at him and scratched him but he'd continue to follow her like the white shadow of a black cat. We were not supposed to have any pets at the Center, and Byeli—that became his new name by then, meaning "white" in Russian and Croatian—was very visible; he went to all the cocktail parties and jumped on the tables for ham and cheese. We had once just thrown his litter box outdoors to air, and in the sand that was scattered, Byeli was making a target spot for his crap just as the director and several business-suited trustees entered to examine whether the art colony was a worthwhile investment. The philanthropic gentry faced a blinking, straining tomcat.

He often visited Tina, who wore heavy paint-smeared black winter coats that dragged on the ground and got pinched by her hiking shoes; she chain-smoked and boozed, painted large yellow canvasses with wall paint—cheaper than oil—and at exhibitions, among her paintings, she had photographs of herself, nude. Byeli played in her apartment on the second floor, inhaling all the noxious vapours, and he once jumped from her window, startling the abstract sculptor below.

He hunted ants. He'd follow an ant, gently press his paw on it, lick it away from its path; disoriented, the ant would run in circles. Late at night he gazed at his ant in the crack on the floor. He poked his paw in the stream of our dripping faucet before he went to sleep atop a circular coat rack.

In the early spring we took him for walks, his head peeping out of Jeanette's red jacket below her chin. Near the post office were several emaciated men with pink, hollow eyes, confounded, leaned on their walking sticks, and when they saw Byeli, a shadow of joy lit their faces, and when we left, they still stood there, smiling, as though the Pope had just given them a blessing.

After my fellowship was over, Jeanette and I drove to Nebraska to live in a cabin in the woods. Byeli stretched out on the dashboard and whenever he noticed a dog in a car, he growled and hissed.

Sometimes I'd catch Jeanette doing 85–90 mph. One of our back tires blew before an exit ramp in Iowa. I tried to change it, but the wheel was rusted because of the Cape Cod salt and sand. We noticed a Tow & Tire several hundred yards away, but I walked to a gas station that was closer. The attendant told me he couldn't change the tire for me, but a friend of his, who lived 15 miles away, would.

"How about the Tow & Tire place?"

"No, no, you don't want to deal with them. They are crooks."

I went to the crooks. They towed our pickup for free and changed our tire for four bucks. Neighbouring mechanics often have terrible epithets for each other—the worse one speaks about another, the better the other must be. That's nearly a rule.

Jeanette bought a can of diet cat food with extra fibre for Byeli, who had steamed in the pickup—it was a hot day.

"Are you crazy? He doesn't need to diet," I said.

"Sure he does; he's getting no exercise in here."

"All the fibre means is faster digestion. He'll need to crap right away!"

"But see, he loves it!" Byeli crunched the brown, red and green mini-pretzels.

"At least we should have a litter box," I said.

"We can always stop and let him do it in sand. He'll ask."

Just then Byeli began to scratch the rubber on the floor, perched himself conically, with his thick orange seal tail raised and trembling.

"Stop the car!" Jeanette shouted and pushed Byeli from his spot to delay him.

"Let the poor guy do it!" I said.

"Stop it! I don't want any cat stink in here; you can never wash it out! Stop it!"

"I am stopping, don't you see!"

"You are taking too long."

"So? It's you who didn't want a litter box in here."

Byeli's tongue hung out as if he were a dog. Ordinarily it was pink but now it was red.

"He's thirsty too. You can't expect him to go without water for a whole day," I said.

I stopped the pickup on the shoulder of an exit ramp on I-80. Byeli jumped out and sniffed the dry soil disdainfully—couldn't compare to his fine beach sand at Cape Cod. He ran into the field and hid in a hole with crumbling soil. We called him but he wouldn't come out—for a while. He didn't use the soil. Jeanette and I kneeled in the field along the shoulder and scratched the soil with our fingers, throwing it up behind us, to set an example. But he only waited for us to get over it.

His tongue was red-scarlet, his breath extremely short, his nose dry, his pupils thin, and his eyes criss-crossed. "He's dying of thirst," we both said and took him to a gas station.

I poured water over Byeli's fur; much of it slid right over it and some shrank into round drops. He refused to lick his fur and panted faster and faster. We tried milk. Byeli drank a cupful, but his tongue still hung out rabidly. At a rest area we took Byeli to a young fir tree, and scratched the soil for him, to set a paradigm. He ran away into the field, over the fence.

"He's leaving us!" Jeanette shouted.

"I don't blame him."

"I know. You blame me."

"That's right."

"I am sick and tired of your complaining. Do you want a divorce?" she shouted.

"I am considering it."

I was reminded of a French couple, a doctor and her husband, an architect, who had quarrelled on a steep ascent of the Inca trail, decided to divorce, and asked me to witness it. Several days afterwards, I had run into them on the descent to Machu Picchu, and they were married again.

"Asshole," Jeanette said.

Byeli jumped the fence, ran to another fir, and dug a hole in the dark red soil. All tensed up, he produced steamy sticks which piled atop each other like firewood.

Our marriage was saved.

Byeli brushed the soil over the hole from all the sides, building a mound as if over a dear friend's grave.

We moved into a cabin in the hills, surrounded by oaks and a narrow creek. At night our kerosene lamp tired our eyes, and a little rechargeable solar-powered lamp was a nuisance to keep on our shoulder to read. We pumped drinking water, and for showers we used a black water tank perched on a tree. We cooked on a wood-burning stove. Before us, a bachelor who'd taken a dozen years to get a 4.0 undergraduate degree had lived there. He had watched cattle for several ranchers, repaired fences, ridden horses in cattle drives, watched birds, sent his sighting reports to the Audubon Society, read history, kept deer hunters off the hills—and had just gone to a law school in Texas. Outside the cabin, under a roof extended to make an open shack, a black cat, Jezebel, nursed her three black kittens, all males, on neatly piled firewood. The females hadn't passed their swimming exams; the future lawyer said he had drowned them. In fact, he had clubbed them.

According to the country custom, the cats were not supposed to enter the house, to not get spoiled. One hazy-blue-eyed kitten hissed, one purred, and one, a longhair ball, rubbed its back against your palm. We named them, respectively, Hitler, Stalin, and Churchill.

When Mike, an Australian Blue Heeler, a crafty dog who stole neighbours' shoes, came close to the woodpile, Jezebel clawed him. She also flared up at a horse who brought down his head a little too close—she flew at his mouth and the horse swung back, startled.

In the beginning of June we brought Byeli to the cabin. Jezebel at once made a lot of his white fur fly and cut into his right eyelid. By cat law, he was supposed to leave and he did start off into the woods. We locked him in the cabin. They growled at each other through the mosquito screen. At night Byeli changed his song; a sorrowful tomcat voice came out, wailing and lamenting, cajoling. His throat vibrated in strange frequencies, possessed by various demons, souls of future cats to be born through his sex—as if they all clamoured to be released from the prison of being, his scrotum. He clawed at the door and windows. Although her kittens were not two months yet, Jezebel responded with her high-frequency, gentle, questioning cries, but if he approached, she growled and leapt at the mosquito door. He came to us upstairs, emitting the possessed cries, jumped on Jeanette, and gripped her shin with his canines. She screamed and kicked him.

To make a studio with electricity, we cleared an old farmhouse, belonging to Jeanette's uncle Al, who had recently got married for the first time at the tender age of 62. Al had no use for the house filled with spiders dead in their own cobwebs, mousetraps, mouse skeletons. A whole room with a creaking floor was filled with *Scientific American*, *National Geographic*, and *Angus* magazines. If I had thought I could stereotype farmers as uneducated hicks, I was wrong. Of the five brothers, who were all ranchers, four had master's degrees, and only Al hadn't obtained any degrees, but obviously read and knew a lot. He enjoyed the reputation for being the smartest brother, partly because he hadn't gone to college and mostly because he hadn't married—and that he married at 62, nearly on his deathbed with cirrhosis of the liver, could not be taken for a dumb move either.

Mouldy clothes covered his floors: army suits, jeans, white gentlemanly summer suits, all moth-eaten. Heaps contained Jim Beam bottles, matches, bullets, heaters, burners with melted wires, green TV sets with missing legs, aluminum antennas with dozens of arms thrown every which way—like a dancing Shiva gone mad. In the yard there were sinks, cabinless pickups, guns with rotted handles, dilapidated barns through whose cracks winds imitated owls' mating cries, an old baler, a rusted tractor with front wheels only a foot apart, an overturned green car without wheels.

But not everything was the past there. On the south side of the yard there was a corn-filled crib, a new John Deere tractor, and out in the field nearly two hundred cows, all worked by one tanned, white-haired man in boots and a rolled leather hat, pipe-smoking, resembling a retired Marlboro man. When I met him, I couldn't understand his slurred Nebraska speech, nor could he understand my mélange. But that didn't prevent us from having a conversation about World War II.

Jeanette and I had burnt most of the junk in the yard, peeled off multiple layers of wallpaper, painted the walls, and got the water going in the bathroom; but there was no septic tank and so we used an outhouse, not the most cheerful chapter; resident wasps stung me, always twice in a quick row.

I took Byeli—Byeli didn't stink—to the new place and he bit me. I couldn't kick him because I was afraid he'd run away. He tore out of my hold. I wanted to catch him, and instead of dodging me, he surprised me with a quick leap, tearing deep into my right palm. I bled profusely; my hand got swollen at once as though a snake had bitten me.

Byeli disappeared from the farm during our continued repairs before he could have developed a sense of home. Although we roamed the hills, we heard nothing of him. We went to our nearest neighbour, Holzer, a rancher who, as the rumour had it, trapped coyotes, and considered it his duty to kill any cats and dogs crossing his path. His pickup had three rifles hung in the back.

We drove to the backyard past several bales of hay. Large dogs barked and a boy of about twelve greeted us.

"Have you seen a white tomcat?" Jeanette asked.

"Yeah, sure thing," answered the boy. "He was here yesterday, in the barn."

His father came out, and we repeated the question.

"Oh yes, I've seen him. He's in the ditch half a mile up the road, dead."

"Are you sure? A white tomcat with creamy peach points and fluffy tail?" gasped Jeanette.

"That's him! If you go up to where the alfalfa ends, you'll see him," the neighbour said, glad to be of assistance.

We drove out and Jeanette cried.

Along the dirt road in the green ditch we saw nothing, but over the barbed wire fence of rotting oak posts, we saw a patch of white, bright in the sun, amidst disked soil. We stepped over the fence and neared the cat. It was pure white—no darkening, slightly Siamese, points on the nose, ears, paws and tail.

"Thank God, it's not Byeli!" shouted Jeanette. I was happy too, but the sight of a dead tomcat was not a cheerful one: the white stranger lay on the soil, his four paws up as if in defense against the sky, his mouth opened a little with black blood in the corners and in the slits of his eyes. Swarms of black flies with purplish-green, radiant wings, buzzed around.

"Clubbed to death!" Jeanette said.

That night Byeli leaped through the back-door mosquito screen, a high jump considering that the rotting porch had collapsed as we'd moved the cast-iron tub out there to read in, under the sun. Covered in thistles, he jumped on the bed and sucked the blanket— his response to any trauma. As an early orphan with Siamese traits, he was a passionate blanket sucker all his life.

Byeli couldn't have much society around, and he had always hankered for cat society. At the Fine Arts Work Center he had followed every cat, begging it to play with him—always snubbed, swallowing saliva, with his blue eyes criss-crossing in intense psychological distress.

We left him at the farm and slept at the cabin. Whenever our pickup pulled out of the yard, he ran after us, down the lane, crying, for half a mile. And when he heard us coming, he ran towards us, and once the pickup slowed down, leaped through the window inside to rub his forehead against us, crying. He rubbed against our legs as we got out and rolled in the dirt, getting all dusty and grey.

Hissing Hitler had disappeared. Byeli and Churchill got along grand, the former licking the latter's fur for hours. Of course, Byeli now and then bit Churchill, and whenever Churchill felt the biting was coming, he tiptoed away. Since three tomcats in one place were too many, we gave Churchill to a couple of friends of ours in Omaha, a marriage counsellor and his girlfriend, a theology major. Churchill was fed on rations, according to some formula, once a day, at 8:30 in the morning precisely. What lay in store for Churchill was declawing, castration, and vegetating—he probably wouldn't even be allowed to grow fat in compensation. One Friday, while Paula was bringing in health-food groceries and Jim writing down the exact mileage it took to drive to the Co-op and back, Churchill ran out through the open door and never came back. If you are thinking of giving a kitten to a marriage counsellor, my advice is: don't.

Byeli often went to the armchair where Churchill used to sleep, sniffed Churchill's hairs, and cried desolately.

The sleek, thin, and shiny Stalin, like an Egyptian junior god, noiselessly snuck around the farmhouse. He passed his boyhood catching grasshoppers. Every five minutes he'd leap through the screen door and crunch his green grasshopper; the antennae and astronomical eyes on the creatures didn't impel him towards mercy at all.

Every morning when I came into the office, I saw fur, blood and animal shit on the floor. Byeli slaughtered gophers, mice, rats, birds and young rabbits who all shat in fear of death. Byeli even ate some years-old mice with rat poison in them and got sick, his tongue purple: he vomited, ate grass and recovered.

Byeli and Stalin began to bring in a mouse a day, each. Byeli once played with a mouse for an hour without killing it and when Stalin wanted to join in, Byeli attacked him. We locked up Byeli so Stalin would get to play some, but Stalin wouldn't touch the mouse. Neither would Byeli when we let him out. With an offended, dignified aura, he sat atop the *Concise Oxford Dictionary* on the bookshelf, and wouldn't even look at the mouse.

Late at night Byeli brought in a rat, tossed him around, bit him, stuck his claws into him; we closed the bedroom door so he wouldn't bring the rat in there. Stalin caught a squealing mouse that had a talent for climbing the wall, sometimes two feet high before falling.

In the morning as we drank our Colombian supremo, from beneath the armchair crawled a brown blood-encrusted mouse. Then out crawled the rat, swollen like a frog, and moving more with his body than limbs, snailing a trail of thin pus and blood. We swept him and the mouse outside. It seems the tomcats thought that since we had interfered in their gaming, we wanted to eat. They paid their rent by bringing us animals in prime condition for eating.

They kept bringing in all kinds of gophers and shrews until they finally understood that we didn't want to eat, and they kept their trophies to themselves, hidden in the barn.

Time and again Byeli chased quick-footed Stalin, treed him or followed him into holes and burrows.

I am no believer in dreams, but as my wife and I saw Byeli's paw caught in the horizontal cellar door—he had most likely chased Stalin and knocked down the opened door leaning against the wall—I recalled the dream: a three-legged white cat trying to enter my teepee. He now cried, his pupils large. Jeanette wept when she saw that his crushed left foot was flat and wide like a spatula. We had been gone for a day—watching movies in Sioux City—and he must have been stuck for at least several hours, trying to get out of the pinch. To console him, we fed him steak. He gulped a whole pound and wanted more. The following morning we took him to the vet, who amputated two of his toes. The other two recovered. The handicap didn't prevent him from taking his manly trips. We were surrounded by grassland and hills, with our nearest human neighbour one mile away. The stretches between cottonwoods along a creek and the oaks and cedars on the hills were long; coyotes, minks, bobcats roamed the terrain imperceptibly and a horned owl supervised them. Whether Byeli would survive his trips was always a question, but we let him be a natural cat—better to be Alexander the Great and die young than be nobody and die old.

Byeli began to spray. He angled his rear upwards, fluffed up his tail, shook his ass in a quick vibration, and sprinkled the door from the outside, throwing up the piss nearly two yards high. I thought all tomcats did it that way but, later, observing Stalin's much more direct way—puddle formation—I realized that Byeli was a stylist. Perhaps a French name, Neige, would have suited him best after all. Byeli assailed mostly my typewriter and bills. When I filed taxes, my yellowed W-2s stank of cat urine. What the hell, I thought, we should have an organic government.

He destroyed dozens of envelopes and piles of photocopies of my articles and stories—perhaps he was a good editor—and generally was a serious setback to my writing, so much so that I am now trying to recover the money by writing about that nasty enemy of literary ambition. I know that the cat is the symbol of libraries and night reading. Many sophisticated bookstores have black and white cats silently seated somewhere among the shelves, adding the aura of mystery to book reading. But let me tell you, these are no tomcats; most of them are castrati, the promoters of culture. A library cat has nothing but disdain and horror for country tomcats. I can attest to it. Byeli and Stalin once held a discussion at the threshold to our bedroom, over my black shoes. Lyrically shaking his tail, Byeli scented the shoes with a powerful message that Stalin was under no circumstances ever to enter that room again. Stalin sniffed at the shoe, moaned and humbly emitted a shot of his ink, printing a petition, which said, Please, Your Highness, allow me to pass through to the bathroom to drink water. I will be obedient. Byeli came back to my shoe, meowed, his eyes criss-crossed with indignation that his authority was flouted, and sprinkled a criss-crossing stream, which said, Application denied. Fuck off.

Two months afterwards I strolled in these shoes through a used bookstore in Omaha, an overpriced one next to a cappuccino store, with backgammon and chess in the back, and with a quiet black and white cat, amazingly clean, wide-eyed, right at the entrance. The former female or male followed me, and as I looked at Heinrich Böll's *Group Portrait with a Lady*, it sniffed my shoes. I moved to another shelf and the cat followed me; it even growled, low, something you'd never expect of a bookstore cat. It must have finally deciphered the conversation that had taken place between Stalin and Byeli. The cat suddenly ran away from me and hid beneath the cash register.

Byeli's trips took more and more time as he groped through the blond catless countryside of the fall in search of sex. The drought made the overgrazed grass look like a yellow crewcut; the hills looked like sand dunes of the Sahara—they had been sand dunes as recently as ten thousand years ago. As strong winds blasted, the horizon softened, unlined in a brown haze, while red-tailed hawks frolicked, surfing on the crests of the winds, far more graceful and elegant than the bald eagles several miles north, above the Missouri, near the bluffs of South Dakota. The flight of an eagle compared to the flight of a red-tail is like the clanking of the New York subway compared with the buttressed glide of the Parisian métro. In that deserted landscape, we didn't know whether Byeli had scraped up any sex for himself.

Hoping to make procreation easier for him, we brought Jezebel to the farm. Byeli hounded and beat her so she hid in holes under the house, but the tide turned and she defended herself ferociously; she even began to attack him. He sat around her on the porch, striking poses, semi-profiles, obviously trying to look charming, blinking, but to no avail. She scratched him up so that he nearly lost his eye and he got an abscess on his front leg, larger than a Ping-Pong ball. We tried to pierce it, having shaved the hair on it, but his skin was amazingly tough. He licked it and licked it until it popped.

We put Jezebel three miles away from us in a barn next to a house of a retired businessman, an Exxon man, who chainsawed nearly one thousand trees, mostly elms, during the summer. He lorded over and humiliated the landscape until the fall, when his blood vessels, shaped like tree roots, burst in his brain, sympathetically avenging the trees.

Mike, the Australian Blue Heeler, lived at the barn, and together with a beagle female, ganged up to chase Jezebel. She had whipped them both piecemeal when she had her kittens, but now, her courage was diminished. She disappeared. A severe December brought wind from the north across the Missouri. We couldn't find her anywhere.

Karma in animal lives has a tendency to be over-reactive, just as in ours. The female beagle, Mike's companion, was shot by her owners on account of being female (and not a cat chaser, her true downfall). Mike, her blue boyfriend, listlessly sat and didn't even seek out cats to chase. Jeanette got him company from her voluntary work at Winnetoon Village Mini Mall Co-op, which offered health food, massages, and gourmet coffee. A customer gave her two Doberman/Blue Heeler pups. Having clubbed to death six pups, the owner grew nauseated and couldn't club any more, and thus were those two spared.

We let them stay on our front porch with Mike, although they all chased our cats, except for Byeli, who stuck his claws in Mike's nostrils so deep that he couldn't get them out—Mike ran and shook him all around the yard, and Byeli hung by the bleeding nose before he fell off with bits of grey hair on his red claws. The male pup ranged too far and disappeared. The coyotes ate him.

Every night the coyotes surrounded our yard. Most of them howled but some barked—they must have interbred with dogs. Mike marked his territory and barked so viciously that the coyotes must have taken him for a whole pack and stayed farther away. He even broke into the outhouse and smeared some human smells over his fur, and so, equipped with war colours, with human authority, he dared cross his narrowly circumscribed boundary into the coyote-land, like a West Berliner with a diplomatic passport crossing through the Brandenburg Gate into East Germany.

One night we heard a shrill cat-like, mating sound, but louder, shriller, with a tremolo.

"Come out, the coyotes are killing Stalin!" Jeanette shouted.

We ran out with a flashlight and screamed to chase them away. We regretted we had no gun—we were usually opposed to shooting coyotes. Our cats showed up. Stalin crawled into a hole beneath the house, and Byeli, electromagnetized, sat on a board of the collapsed back porch.

The coyotes were killing a fawn—that's how the farmers assessed our report of shrill cries. But in the morning we couldn't find a trace of the skeleton; the coyotes must have finished everything right on the spot or dragged the remains away.

During the severest cold spell, Byeli was gone. We began to count him for dead too, but early one morning he jumped through the first back door—the second one was closed—and clawed and cried. He was cold, shiny, thin. He rubbed his arched back against us, poked his large head under our chins, purred his deep purr into our ears, licked our noses raspily so that they turned red, and sucked the blankets and the sweater on me, plucking the threads. For several days he slept, purred, sucked the blanket, and went with me to the basement where we kept a large furnace going. Every morning instead of praying, I started a fire in the furnace with paper and small wood, throwing in large pieces of redwood afterwards—and as flames grew, red and yellow and evasive, I felt more and more warm and alert; it was better than coffee, though of course coffee followed, ground in a little Krups mill and boiled in a fifty-cent Goodwill aluminum percolator, with Byeli still at my side, rubbing against my ankles and howling for canned tuna.

He often sat in front of the electric heater in the bathroom—the furnace duct to the bathroom was rusted and collapsed—basking in the red heat, tilting his body against the base of his thick tail, his eyes closing and opening slowly, his head sinking. Now and then he slept on the large furnace, where possums used to sleep before we let Mike live with us. Mike killed the possums, leaving their bodies to rot in the yard for weeks before he took several bites from them, and always found them disappointing. The corpses rotted for several months into the spring.

In March near the deserted tree-hater's house, we ran into a thin black cat. It was Jezebel. She cried as she tried to climb us, with her large claws digging into our jeans. At once we took her to our pickup. We had some doubts as to whether it was the same mother cat, but as she farted her extraordinarily stinky farts and took a crap right on Holzer's driveway, our doubts disappeared—she had crapped precisely there in the fall.

Byeli, a twenty-pound thug, attacked her at once. He was in heat and so was she, and so was a little scraggly country cat we'd taken under our wing and named The Forum for Thought. A student of mine at Nebraska Indian Community College at Santee asked me whether I could give her two tomcats, and to get them, Jeanette and I visited a farmer with a vicious Doberman and many little cats that hid in a small barn. We offered them food, and, while we were catching a little tabby with patches of orange, the Doberman opened his jaws and closed them over it to swallow it. The farmer kicked the dog, the jaws opened up, and we bagged the cat. It was a female. She had two personalities, one indoor, one outdoor; they switched precisely on the threshold of our house. Outdoors she hid in holes, climbed trees, hissed and spat, and responded to no calls. Indoors, she purred several purrs at once, choking with joy, on your neck right into your ears, trying to enter into your mind. Her growth was stunted, but it still didn't prevent her from joining in the general heat. Stalin and Byeli took turns impregnating her, while she growled. Then Byeli jumped Jezebel. She refused Stalin, her son. The howling and growling, spitting, shouting was too much for us, so we threw them all out.

In one day Byeli repeatedly jumped the little Forum for Thought and Jezebel. Stalin, who had for months adored and gently licked the little one, preparing her for himself, was soon forbidden to jump her. He watched on as Byeli did. Byeli also raped Stalin's mother in front of his eyes. But Stalin's troubles weren't over, because Byeli jumped him too, grabbing him by the neck. Stalin growled and cried, his eyeballs popping. After laying everything in sight, Byeli slept solidly for a day and then took a trip.

We heard all kinds of reports. He had visited Alfred's farm—a pig farmer a mile east of us—two loud dogs notwithstanding, whipped a resident tomcat, and caught several rats, piling them at the entrance of an empty barn that used to house cows. Nowadays cows stay outdoors even in hailstorms, and the farmers take it to be good for the cows—they grow stronger and fatter that way; and if a cow dies of pneumonia, well, that's less bother than building and maintaining barns, now abandoned to rats amidst mouldy corn. Driving past Alfred's pig pens—you could tell the season by how large the piggies were—we often asked about Byeli. "Yessir, he was here a couple of days ago."

I saw Byeli behind the town bar, seven miles away, in Center. He was the only white cat in the neighbourhood, so there was no doubt that it was him. Byeli leaped into a shed and wouldn't respond to my calls.

"He's left us," said Jeanette. "That's a tomcat for you, a terrible pet."

Two nights later he jumped through the first door and, though the second was closed, shoved it open with a bang. He ran to us and pushed his nose under our chins and purred. Jeanette brushed his hair and he bared his long teeth, relaxing his jaws. We fêted him with chicken livers.

In the litter box he stood upright, with his front legs leaning straight on the tall edge, and he was so full of imperial dignity that he didn't bother to bury his crap. The little Forum for Thought, who monitored the action, buried it for him. She followed him around like a suspicious cop.

We bathed him to get rid of the new fleas, but when his fur dried, there seemed to be more. He ran out, rolled in the weeds—he knew the right kind—and the fleas were gone. He slept in the sunshine near the window, his paws crossed one over another; or, as a true stylist, he slumbered with one of his paws in the pool-table pocket, his head on the cue ball for a pillow; or with all four legs spread wide, his head hanging down from the table, his balls showing shamelessly, his long and muscular body stretched. He looked like a bodybuilder.

Time and again he yawned, expressing pure boredom, some kind of existential ennui. But ever since he had learned about sex, he couldn't be bored for long. Although Jezebel was pregnant, several days before she was due, he howled at her his lewd propositions. She spat back at him and meowed in alarm. He grabbed her neck with his long teeth, and she accepted the game, lifted her behind, pushing her backwardly stretched paws against the floor, alternately, now one, now another, claws sliding and screeching. She growled and Byeli did his thing, crouching over her. She cried more and more and in orgasms she tore away, her claws sparking at him. Instead of withdrawing, he'd run after her, slap her, and jump her again. To have some quiet, we threw them outdoors, but it went the same way. We separated Byeli from her, and he throated strange, desperate, muted howls, and pissed over the ending of my novel about the decline of communism. To save my manuscript, I let him approach her again. He must have jumped her several hundred times in four days and nights. She couldn't take it any more and we separated them in earnest. For a break, he attacked Stalin, cleaving his skin; Byeli had no need of trees for sharpening claws. Stalin sat bleeding under the bed. No doubt Byeli would have killed Stalin if we hadn't separated them. After all that, Byeli just collapsed from exhaustion.

Even before attacking Jezebel, Byeli had been in poor shape. We had found him on the road, near our mailbox, three-quarters of a mile away from our house. He just stood there on the road and cried, sunken, dirty, lacking will. If we had continued driving, I believe he would have let us drive over him. His fur was gluey. He limped. "Something terrible has happened to him," Jeanette had said. I thought that he limped because his two-toed foot couldn't take so much running; it was swollen.

During his gradual recovery he got those sexual seizures. So when he collapsed after the orgy, he really collapsed. I was away to a pow-wow and a conference on Native American education in Bismarck. On my way up, the towns were shrouded in brown clouds of soil-dust. The pow-wow took place in a no-smoking ballroom of the Radisson Hotel. When I came back, Byeli's balls were swollen and blue. His whole back was swollen with abscesses. He couldn't urinate; water dripped out of his penis, drop by drop, when he tried to walk. He couldn't jump, he didn't purr, but his eyes were alert. When I came home, Jeanette said, he livened up. He began to recover quickly, but to be safe, we took him to the vet, who examined him under anaesthesia. His blood and temperature were normal.

At home, Byeli strolled, his fur began to look good, he slept, but grew bored and constantly begged to be let out. We forcibly kept him inside for two more days, giving him the pink liquid antibiotics through an eyedropper. Some of the pink stayed on the fur on the sides of his mouth.

It was springtime and on a sunny day we let him step outside to sit on a plank of wood. We would keep an eye on him so he wouldn't go away. Jeanette filled a large bottle with powdered milk and walked to the corral on the other side of the house to feed two orphan calves. They were orphans because their mothers hadn't licked them at birth and they didn't smell like any mother's saliva. The orphans' ears, sticking straight out of their heads parallel with the ground, were wet from sucking. After the calves had finished sucking the milk from the large bottle-nipple with their round grey tongues, they nudged each other under the stomachs, as they would their mothers had they had them, and proceeded to suck on each other's members. Jeanette called me out, and while we laughed at the calves, Byeli left.

"Well, let him," Jeanette said. "This warm weather is good for him."

I agreed.

Three days later, in the premature dark of heavy clouds, right before a storm, he suddenly showed up, with sheet lightening trembling behind him between the earth and the sky, accompanied by growling thunder and shuddering of windowpanes. He was silent. He looked quite well. I brushed him the whole evening. He purred, looking me in the eye, and didn't suck the blanket. He nudged his wet nose under my chin, and rubbed his forehead against my ears. In the morning he took a look at his children; there were ten kittens nursing between two mothers. The kittens switched mothers and the mothers didn't care: a communist upbringing. He jumped in, trying to grip Jezebel by her nape, to have sex amidst the family. She wouldn't go for it. His children didn't even greet him. He was not needed.

He sprinkled an armchair before the door, with his tail trembling, and he cried with a certain degree of charm. He wanted out. "Why do we put up with this?" Jeanette asked.

In the clear morning we let him outdoors. On the fourth day of his renewed absence, Jeanette said he probably wouldn't make it this time. I went into my room; Stalin began to growl. Stalin now mostly lived in a large empty barn, but whenever it was windy, the hooting of the wind through the cracks terrified him and he came home. (When I printed out a rough draft of this, Stalin stared, his tail's hairs standing out under an electromagnetic spell: as if Byeli's ghost would leap out and sink his claws into Stalin's skin and blood.) Byeli jumped through the high door. Jeanette shouted, "Byeli!" I ran out to see, to be happy, because Byeli was home. But lo, there was a terrible stench with him; his back legs and tail were brown and black with blood, pus, dirt, shit. We washed him with a towel and soap; he cried and bit Jeanette. I held him by the scruff of the neck, surprised that he was light, that he offered no resistance, that there was no strength in him. I laid him on the floor gently. He wanted to drink the soapy water. I ran to get him the clean water, but he had no strength to drink any more. There was a terrible fear in his eyes. A big black and blue hole was in one of his legs; perhaps a coyote had bitten him or a horned owl pierced the muscle. His hair on that leg was almost gone, and when you pulled the skin it stayed up.

"My God, he's dying! He came home to see us before he dies!" Jeanette cried.

She had so often said that, whenever he was hurt, but now I feared she was saying the truth.

"Gangrene," I said.

The fear in Byeli's eyes made me feel how empty my stomach and my arteries and lungs were; his fearful eyes followed me. There had never been much fear there, and now, nothing but vast fear. In his large pupils he begged for something, for help; he wanted to be brushed and comforted; perhaps he knew he was dying and wanted to die with love. But it was close to five o'clock and the vet would leave after five, so we rushed to him.

As we put Byeli on the white metal examination table, he shrieked. Whrow! His eyes were large and he wailed with such resistance and despair that I turned sick from that voice. The last thing he wanted now was the table where his toes had been cut off, thermometers stuck up his ass, syringes in his muscles, scrapers in his ears. We were leaving with that cry and his eyes on us, as if we were abandoning him forever.

And we were, although the vet told us there was a chance he would live.

A day later when Jeanette came home from work, she wept. "Byeli died at the hospital last night, around midnight."

I said the conventional words, "He lived a full, good life. It's natural," and, "God gave and God took away."

I picked him up at the vet's. He came in a carton, the whole package amazingly light. Jeanette and I dug a hole in the ground, struggling to cut through cedar roots. I took him out of the box. His eyes were half open and there was a blue film over them, bluegrey, and you couldn't distinguish between the pupil and the iris. I touched the short hair on his head. Jeanette didn't want to touch him because she wanted to remember him warm. He was frozen and stiff in death, neither peaceful nor dignified, neither tormented nor joyful, but dead. A thing eighteen months old. There was much of him still in his long whiskers and his teeth, which stuck out down on the sides below his sunken cheeks. We put him in the ground, his four paws up against the sky.

No cats showed up for his funeral.

We buried him in the soil and put a log of a collapsed tree over his grave. Many large white birds descended on the brown ploughed soil, where Al had sowed oats behind the grave, and ate before flapping off for the North.

It has taken me a long time to get used to Byeli's not existing because his ghost keeps leaping everywhere for me, and I nearly reach to scratch his forehead, so he can close his criss-crossing eyes and enjoy.

But there he is below the log, with his eyes half open and blue.

Stalin's Perspective

One misty morning a horned owl carried my cat, Little Mama, onto the giant cottonwood in our grove. That's what my wife told me over the phone when I was a thousand miles away.

That an owl would hunt in mist was odd. Once, on the lookout spot over the Niobrara River bleeding mud into the Missouri— at dawn you couldn't see that because of the thick mist—I drove around a mangled deer with a broken antler sprawled on the asphalt, and passed by a dead owl in the gravel. The owl had probably failed to see a pickup in the haze. I made a U-turn to examine the bird. When I could not find the owl among the brown and yellow stones on the roadside, I thought I must have hallucinated because of too little sleep and too much mist, but then I saw it, like a perception puzzle that suddenly fits: brown stripes among black and white spots in semi-circles on the outstretched wings. In the head loomed a hole. One eye lay among stones, independent, perceiving the sky for nobody. I kept the owl because my father-in-law, a biology professor, said he would use it for a lecture, but then he forgot about it, and I forgot about it, and three weeks later in the attic I saw a nation of ants nested in its head, bustling silently.

Now, I had nightmares—cats rising into the sky and falling (it rained cats and cats). I called up Jeanette the first thing next morning, thinking she may have pulled my leg so that I wouldn't be having too much fun in New York while she stayed on a muddy ranch without friends, a TV set, or even modest pleasures like cappuccino. Now she said, "Four cats are gone." When I doubted the story, Jeanette said, "Gail from the post office said the same thing—an owl snatched her cat."

I grieved that my cats had died, but it was better to die in the sky than to get stuck rotting in the mud.

When I returned home, the missing cats—Little Mama, Tesla, Eddy, and Fatso—slept stretched out on the pool table. Happy, I still protested, "Why did you tell me the tall tales?"

"I saw the owl carrying something—and the cats did disappear," Jeanette said. "They must have wandered out to find you."

My happiness increased when Stalin, a tomcat I thought had died, jumped through the window. He had taken a three-month-long trip—that's a tomcat! But to describe what a tomcat he was, I have to backtrack a year and a half.

I met Stalin near a cabin in the woods where Jeanette and I lived after our unemployment benefits ran out. We kept a garden, mostly watermelons, read by kerosene lamps (*National Geographic* and *Audubon* magazines, leftovers from a previous freak resident), and took showers from a black-painted tank of water, which we filled with buckets. Bats lived in our attic, and a pregnant cat in our woodpile ballooned out a batch of five pitch-black kittens. I liked to tickle Stalin, the kitten with the shortest hairs, in the piles of wood where he tried to catch the sun's shadows. He was the first to purr and lie on his back to play with my fingers, his little gums biting me toothlessly. His mother, Jezebel, a speedy cat—once I saw her fly up a wild cherry tree and catch a blissful bird with a cherry in its beak—walked the kittens into the tall grass and wild marijuana. She jumped at a dead mouse and nudged them to imitate her. They did. Then she'd toss the mouse, and they did the same.

When Jeanette got a job as a counsellor and I as an instructor of history on a nearby reservation, we moved to an abandoned ranch house with electricity ready to be hooked up, running water, mounds of junk, mouldy walls to peel and paint, and an outhouse.

An Australian Blue Heeler lived on the ranch and ran after cows, keeping company with the rancher who owned the dilapidated house and lived in the town of seventy-two, six miles away. As soon as Stalin met Ivan, who had been dozing in the sun on the cracking porch, I heard Stalin growl for the first time in his life. Ivan's eyes crossed in surprise before he snapped his jaws and barked. For Stalin, a sad childhood ensued, with a lot of tree climbing.

Stalin knew that I protected him. If I looked at him across the room, he'd start purring and would purr away the whole evening in the happiness of being looked at once. And when I stroked him, a loud purr vibrated.

Light shimmered on Stalin's sleek body. Stalin licked his black fur for hours, for he was quite vain. Even his anus looked spotlessly clean. I gave him an old pork chop, noticing too late that it contained a bone. When I tried to grab the bone away, Stalin leaped out the window and hurriedly chewed the whole thing. The bone stuck in his throat, he choked for half a day, coughing, trembling, and then the bone passed on. Stalin was taken with fevers. I tried to keep him warm in bed, but nothing helped. For a whole week, he shivered, trembled, moaned, and his anus shone all too white. If only something would pass! But nothing came out and in came only milk, because he could never resist milk, not even now on his probable deathbed. On his very worst day, he purred, as though death was a comfortable deliverance.

The bone eventually partly melted and the rest came out, with blood. His insides torn, he failed to regain his appetite for a whole month. He had not grown at all in that month, but his knowledge of the world did: thou shalt not swallow bones.

Stalin was a youngster when he caught his first grasshopper, crunching it in his jaws ostentatiously. The drought had invited a grasshopper plague. Dejected farmers drank beer and discussed the pestilence. Sparrow hawks multiplied and flew a foot or two off the ground along the curves of the rolling hills, like fighter planes, feasting in the air on the meat that sprang from the grass like a blessing. Red-tailed hawks dived from high streams of warm air into the sparse grass, caught bull snakes, and carried them, slowly gaining altitude, while the snakes struggled, sending waves through their bodies to destabilize the hawks. From up high, the hawks would drop bull snakes onto the hard, bald fields, dive after them, and stand breathless, with talons piercing the snakes. When the hawks slowly ascended, the snakes no longer sent waves, but hung limply dead.

Whenever Stalin caught a grasshopper, he jumped back into the room and chewed it in front of me. When I petted him, he proudly bared his canines—instead of four, there were eight. Next to the larger ones, new ones grew, fighting for space out of the same roots, like twin trees, until only four victorious fangs remained, to serve a lifetime.

Stalin had to compete for our affection. Little Mama was determined to be my favourite. She slept on my ear, and when Jeanette came close to me, Little Mama clawed her, as though to say that I needed no wives but her, the cat. When Little Mama realized she couldn't win that one, she learned to like Jeanette, though there was always something insincere in that affair. Little Mama was our smartest cat. She slid the sliding doors, pushed the swing doors, and was always the first to find new cracks and groceries. She constantly talked, in a marvellous medley of whirrs, purrs, cries, squeaks, chirps, gurgles, pleas, and cackles. When I took walks, she followed me into the fields, like a lean red puppy. On the surface she was a grey and black tabby, but when you stroked her hairs against the grain, you saw that her essence was red, and indeed, soon she would give birth to two red and two calico kittens. But before that, one step had to be taken: an orgy. In the true tradition of impoverished rural America, she got pregnant before the time assigned to her. My textbook claims a cat should be seven months before she can conceive, but Little Mama was barely six months when Stalin and a big visiting tabby alternately jumped her, finally uniting in one action, and uniting a little too much: to cap the evening, the visitor raped Stalin.

Although a population boom threatened us, Jeanette brought home another female cat, Smokey. Jeanette, who could not resist picking up an orphan, found her on the bridge over the Missouri. Fortunately, Jeanette's mother took Smokey home to Sioux City.

In the winter, unadventurous Stalin stayed in the basement. Two square yards had eroded out of the foundation, and instead of bricking up the hole, I piled rectangular bales of hay over it, hoping that that would keep the godly elements outside. Cats easily slid through a crack between the hay and the wall, tiptoed over piles of wood sprawled all over the basement, and jumped onto the large furnace with ducts that led to the rooms above. The dusty top of the furnace could stay warm for two days on one load of red elm. As Jeanette and I drove home from a weekend in Omaha, two miles away from home I noticed a black cat running thirty miles an hour. Did he look for us, or was he becoming a regular adventurer, or did Ivan the Terrible send him into exile?

Ivan piled the dead squirrels, rabbits, and possums with their erect penises, in a heap. When male possums faked death, they neither had nor faked erections. You could tell whether a male possum was dead by the stiff erection that strangling had brought on. When I filled the water drum for calves to drink, the bloated animals floated while Ivan wagged his tail and looked at me with his shiny eyes, expecting a compliment. But the scoundrel—who stole my shoes and chewed them as though they were fresh beef, who ate Jeanette's wool sweaters and slept on the roof of our car, did not get a compliment because he had chased Stalin into the hills.

A visiting tabby now and then tortured Stalin, cutting his skin so that Stalin sat under the bed in a puddle of his own blood. Stalin was so subdued that he'd be whipped for life, I thought, so whipped that he wouldn't even dare take a trip. But he did take a worrisomely long trip.

One night during a severe wind chill, I stayed at school to finish assigning the final grades. At ten, when I was ready to go, my pickup would not start. I walked into the gym; there, most of the tribe was playing bingo, oblivious to the winter. My students did not even register me, and a stranger helped me jumpstart the pickup. Since I was concerned that Jeanette would worry, I rushed on the snow-packed and icy roads. I knew every curve, but on one I spun out; the pickup flew over a ditch and crashed into a fence post. I got out, amazed that my neck was all right, the tires were all right, but my eyeballs seemed to freeze in the wind and my moustache and beard became icicles from my steamy breath. Meanwhile, since we did not have a phone—a bulldozer that levelled the driveway cut the line, and it would have cost a grand to get another line—Jeanette had walked to our nearest neighbour, Ganz, a mile away. When I got home (the pickup had easily pulled out of the drift), she was still looking for me in the hills. If I had just stopped by at a bar, would she go out and look for me? Where was the freedom? But then, if I had got stuck, freezing to death . . . At that thought, I heard a specific tomcat's broken cry out of the snow. I fed Stalin crunchies and milk. I made a big fire in the furnace, piling up four big logs and nearly crushing my forefinger. Jeanette came back, and we all snuggled as a happy family of mammals. Jeanette recounted her wanderings in the hills. We concluded that we should get a phone, even though people had lived without phones for seventy thousand years.

In the morning all the pickup tires were flat. The jolt had broken the seals.

Now, although Stalin adored milk, he cowered before his mother Jezebel, before Little Mama, and even before the kittens, his younger half-brothers, daughters, stepsons. Two litters had grown

90

together, shared by two mothers—fat, content, and self-confident. I especially liked one black kitten—a sort of junior Stalin, shiny, sleek, purry. He sat in front of my computer screen, sniffed at the wiring, and slept atop a TV set, which we had just bought. He studied the discharge of static from his paw onto the screen, and stared into the disappearing blue dot when we turned off the set. He once jumped on my keyboard, and it crashed on the floor. Though the damage was almost one hundred dollars, I could not be mad at the young scientist, Tesla. Tesla was the friendliest cat, interested only in electronics and milk—and yet Stalin was afraid even of him.

Among the kittens, Stalin hissed, his body slinking close to the floor and paws stepping gingerly, but you could see that there was a lot of spring in his crouched style. A destroyed panther. I wanted to make a room for him, but Jeanette pointed out that he sprayed too much, especially over her clothes. We often had disagreements as to how to treat the cats. At that time, she got a letter from her ex-boyfriend in Colombia; she read it, and told me that we were invited to visit him in Bogotà. "That's great," I said, and I meant that it was great that she could so freely show a letter relating to her amorous past. I too got a letter from an ex-girlfriend from East Germany who had visited Leningrad, fallen on ice, and broken her leg. I hid the letter and wondered whether I should get a mailbox so I could correspond with old friends peacefully. I forgot to burn the letter, and when Jeanette found it, she was furious.

"Why are you shouting?" I said.

"Because you were hiding it!"

"You get letters from your old men-friends, so why shouldn't I from my women-friends?"

"A letter from my past means only friendship to me, and I am not sure that it does to you. Men are more restless than we are. Just look at our tomcats!"

"You have double standards," I said.

"You do. You are the one who's got something to hide!"

"No, you are just less tolerant—you are proving it right now!—and that's why..." But I believed that she was more honest and more right—and freer—than I was, and I admired and resented that.

"Admit it, you are sick of our living in the country. Let's move!" she said.

And so, on went the quarrel and escalated, and it left such an unpleasant impression that I never replied to the letter, not even when East Germany melted into the West.

From then on, Jeanette did not let Stalin into the house, as if he signified my tomcat side that had to be kept at bay. Stalin lived in the attic of a large deserted red barn, looking out through a small window for me to show up and give him cans of food. He had a lot of scratches in his skin, all over his body and on his nose, and my metal comb got some old crusts out of his hairs and stimulated his skin to regenerate. Sometimes, when the combing excited him so much that his scarlet penis, shiny and pointed, slid out of its sheath, he rolled on his back and took swings at my face, with his long claws out, playfully and viciously trying to scratch me up. As the claws flew by my eyes, they discharged crackling static onto my eyebrows.

Shiny grey ticks grew on him. When I neglected to visit Stalin, the small tick heads ballooned into blood-filled bodies as large as hazelnuts. I tore off the ticks on his tail and forehead, and hammered them against the floor, the damned barn resounding like a tremendous drum, while the blood burst under the rusted hammer. With a pocketknife I scraped off the disembodied tick heads from his skin.

In the summer, Jeanette and I prepared to go to Eastern Europe (Colombia was out): Poland, Czechoslovakia, Hungary, Yugoslavia, but not East Germany. As we packed our Renault—an addition our jobs gave us—to drive to Omaha and catch a plane, Tesla licked the radio antenna. Little Mama, who nursed four sprightly three-week-old babies in a drawer, came out and sniffed at the luggage. She rubbed her arched back against our shins and cackled in a protest. We read in her eyes the knowledge of our betrayal.

When we came back, the cats had disowned us. The kittens fled from us. When they jumped back through the hole in the mosquito screen in the window to get food, I worried about the missing Little Mama until I realized that there were five kittens rather than four—I had mistaken her for one. She was just as small as they, even thinner, and even more humble. She did not know me, or she did and did not trust me. I picked her up but she would not purr, and she continued to look resentful as long as it took us to tame the kittens.

Stalin showed up two weeks later from a trip in the American Siberia. There was a packed quality about him that I saw in bulls: taut muscles amassed around the neck and on shoulders that seemingly slowed down the beast. When he saw me, he growled. I bent to touch him. He screeched and hissed. When Jeanette tried to pet him, he jumped into her shin. If she hadn't worn leather boots, she'd have scars for life. I gave him milk but he wouldn't purr. Next time he came by, I gave him milk, and he let me comb him and pluck his two ticks. I burst the ticks. He looked at me in recognition or forgiveness, and purred. He stayed for a week, sleeping in an unhooked sink.

In Sioux City, Jeanette and I visited her parents—at Jeanette's childhood home, with a For Sale sign stuck in the front lawn (Jeanette joked that her childhood was being sold)—and instead of the parents, found two scared kittens. A month after giving birth to them, Smokey had run out into the street, where a car smashed her jaw. Jeanette's mother took Smokey to the vet. Ken, her husband, did not know about it until he picked up the phone two weeks later.

"You may now pick up Smokey Baldwin."

"Who is Smokey Baldwin?" he asked.

"Why, your cat! It'll be only three hundred and fifty dollars."

Ken, whose calves sold for four hundred and fifty, was mad, or pretended to be. He talked about how he would shoot the cat, burn her with dry ice, but, as a matter of fact, Smokey slept right atop his head almost every night, and he was mighty attached to her, just as a local farmer, Jim, was to his fifteen-year-old sick cat, without knowing it. Jim decided he would shoot the bothersome dirty old cat, and he talked about it in the local bar, to the approval of the ranchers, who all seemed to be routine cat shooters. But after Jim shot his cat, and saw her twitch, and shot her again, he wept for days, recalling what his cat and he had gone through together in the fifteen years. Jeanette and I took advantage of his emotional breakdown to give him three kittens. Anyhow, Smokey came home with a reconstructed jaw and an unreconstructed resentful personality.

When we walked into the home in Sioux City, these two orphans, all hairs on end, flew down the stairs, crashing into a garbage bin in a turn. Jeanette and I took them to our farm.

Sorely deprived of motherly love, the newcomers considered themselves to be little kittens. While Little Mama nursed her new batch, the two Persians licked the kittens and let the kittens lick them—and once they smelled like babies, smugly they crawled to the bosom, a paradise regained, where they could relive their childhoods, revised and improved, if Jeanette and I hadn't felt sorry for the poor mother.

Because the big Persian tabby loved Little Mama, we called him Oedipus, but soon of course his name decayed into Eddy. When Mama's milk ran out, we had her spayed along with her firstborn redhead. After the operation, the redhead had an abnormally loud purr. A hollow space, like a violin belly somewhere in her, augmented the sound.

Eddy liked one adopted sibling, a red tom named Fatso. When I took baths, Fatso walked onto my chest and belly sticking out of the water, and he drank water out of my navel, and nudged his nose under my chin until I shampooed him. I dipped him into the water and washed him. Then Eddy licked him for hours, while Fatso winked at everybody, fully aware that he would shine, fluffy and pretty. But there was a small price he had to pay: Eddy would bite his nape and try to enter him from the rear. They slept together, walked out in the marijuana fields together, and had a genuinely deep attachment, like David and Jonathan in the Bible.

On excess milk, Eddy grew to be a large cat, with a very large head, large eyes, big tail, big body, but short and thick legs and a snub nose.

One late fall dusk, walking over shushing leaves, I scrutinized the bare treetops in the grove. I counted a dozen nests that I hadn't seen before and wondered about the whereabouts of the horned owl. I missed its ominous hoots. And just as I mused about Stalin's absence, he came home looking fierce, a total beast. The females, even his mother, respectfully let him come in and take the first bite of beef liver. I did not believe in his conversion, not even when I heard a lot of screaming in the basement, the woodpile collapsing. I found Stalin puffing, facing four toms ganged up against him. "Our toms are beating on poor Stalin!" I said to Jeanette.

"No, he's beating them. That's a regular monster there!"

The following morning Stalin came across Fatso, who had just tortured Tesla in the basement. Fatso crapped in fright, and while Stalin puzzled over the smells, opening his mouth, lifting his lips in disgust as though to close his nose, Fatso dashed out into the fields. Red, in the yellow grass, he became a prairie fire chased by southern winds. Stalin looked at me smugly—he wanted me to get the picture—and then, ten minutes later, he pursued Eddy up an old ash tree. Eddy fell down the tall tree together with the rotten bark that a red-headed woodpecker had pecked for days. Stalin jumped after Eddy, tree bark and all, and landed atop him in the tall bluegrass. He was biting Eddy's paw and tearing into him in many ways, until I separated them with a stick, but Stalin snuck away and continued to chew Eddy in the basement.

Eddy took more than a month to recover. Not only did he have an abscess, but his skin was torn to the muscles in places. Thick crusts formed over his wounds. Stalin was offended that I took somebody else's side, as though he should not be entitled to a little bit of tyranny after spending a whole childhood in abuse. That I would kick him—the only way to save Eddy's life—that really hurt Stalin.

Once Eddy began to recover, he thrived at sleeping on the bookshelf filled with magazines from all over the world that we subscribed to, to be cosmopolitan in the country. Eddy loved being ill because Jeanette combed him and gave him chicken livers. He trustingly relaxed in her arms, purring and licking her nose, which turned red, while Little Mama purred into my ear. My other ear tuned into a short-wave radio speaker as Radio Zagreb groaned out the news of civil war in Croatia. Slavonia, my native region, was a wasteland, with abandoned cows, horses, pigs, goats, dogs, and cats wandering, and produce rotting in the fields. A woman who walked back to her village to feed her dog was shot.

Eddy was an extremely nervous and timorous cat. If I looked at him sternly, he'd run and hide in a boot. He must have known that I still protected Stalin.

One thing amazed Jeanette and me. No female cats, although some were more than a year old, got pregnant anymore. Jeanette explained that Little Mama—who, though spayed, retained the status as the dominant female—could not emit the heat signals and smells that would allow other females to go into heat. And so nobody went into heat, until Little Mama lost dominance to Jezebel, who got pregnant on the neighbour's farm a mile away. I theorized that Stalin, no longer interested in sex but only in violence, did not allow

96

any toms to go into heat. Anyway, after Jezebel, the two fourteen-month-old females, Charlotte and Passion, got pregnant, and gave birth to a whole batch of red and calico cats. That none were black proved my point that the dominant Stalin no longer cared for sex, and that Fatso, the largest red tom, was not exclusively gay.

Stalin did not like the smell of our farm with all the little kittens, and he was gone for a whole season.

When he came back, before you knew it, he was flying after Eddy up the old ash tree. This time there was no bark to give way because the tree was now dead and bald. In desperate courage, Eddy jumped from the tree onto the roof of the two-storey house. Stalin, right after him, in a sort of reckless backhand jump, landed on the roof and pursued Eddy to the other end, where Eddy, nearly sliding off, hung by the aluminum gutter. Stalin crouched on the raspy shingles, taking swings at the screaming Eddy. After four hours, Eddy fell to the ground, amazed to be alive. Stalin stayed on the roof for the night. When Jeanette took Eddy indoors, Eddy still trembled. He took a look at his paw, saw that it wasn't too bad, just a little bloody. He stretched—all the bones were fine—and started purring. If he had managed to survive this one, he must have thought, he could survive anything. He was truly born again. Now he grew to be a prosperous and well-adjusted cat.

Stalin snuck around trying to get a definitive bite of Eddy, but Eddy was clever. He realized that Stalin had one big failing: an absolute fear of dogs. Eddy began to sleep on the rotting front porch, Ivan's staunchly defended territory, where Stalin did not trespass. Just as Stalin's purpose in life was to torture Eddy, Ivan's was to torture Stalin. Giving protection to Eddy was Ivan's way of hurting Stalin.

Stalin now took to beating Fatso. Stalin's claws shut Fatso's eye for two weeks, and even after that, it was bloodshot and its eyelid black-red. His paw, too, was chewed up but did not develop an abscess. When Stalin once ran after Fatso, taking a bite here and there, Ivan ran out after Stalin, while Jeanette shouted, "Bravo, Ivan!" After that, Fatso too slept on the front porch, a couple of yards away from Ivan, purring all day long in the sun. He did not even want to go inside, where vicious mothers would attack him.

It was a rainy fall. Drinking cold ones, farmers took bets as to whether the drought had finally broken. Our sporty Renault, low to the ground, got stuck in the mud and lost a wheel bearing over a rock. The pickup with rear wheel drive also kept getting stuck, while the low sky kept drizzling. Another piece of the foundation caved in. Wet mortar from the ceiling beneath a leak in the roof crumpled and made a pile next to the entrance. Wet wood burned slowly, and the crowd of cats refused to go out and fought over the litter box. Jeanette and I put out ads to give away kittens and asked neighbours to adopt the older cats, while we would keep Little Mama and Eddy.

One morning I honked to tease Ivan. The high pitch made him howl in the same frequency; he howled as though keeping a surrounding gang of coyotes at bay. Jeanette and I were off to scout out Minneapolis, to see whether we'd like to live in the city.

While we were gone, Ivan the Blue Heeler hung around the Ganzs' uninvited, eating cat food, and probably chasing Stalin, until Sonny Ganz, the old farmer, shot Ivan in the head—he said he did not know that the dog belonged to anybody—and threw his body into his garbage dump in a small canyon.

"I can't stand it here anymore," Jeanette said. "How can they be so cruel?"

While Jeanette grieved for Ivan, she still hated Stalin for all the suffering he had brought upon our cats. She was glad that he had been away for months, and hoped that he was dead. But Ganz's wife told us that a big black tom came to their farm and killed their month-old kittens and their mother. He'd torn the skin off her sides. I did not believe the story, but Jeanette did.

One warm evening, as we were sorting through our papers, Stalin snuck in. We thought it was Tesla grown bigger, so we paid no attention until Stalin flew into Eddy. Eddy screamed and crapped, while Jeanette kicked Stalin out, and closed the door. When he got in through a window crack in the bathroom and tried again to slice Eddy, Jeanette grabbed a pipe wrench and hit Stalin several times. I tore the wrench out of her hands and shouted at her, while Stalin came back, puffing and looking for Eddy, who was hiding in a boot. I guided Stalin out and closed the door. Jeanette swore she would kill Stalin, and I that I would give Eddy to the animal shelter if she dared to touch Stalin again. After a bad quarrel, I rushed to the basement to give Stalin milk, to console him, and to apologize.

I felt that if I did not show Stalin a bit of kindness, he would die of sorrow. I stroked him. He growled and purred at the same time. That he would growl was a given and that he purred was a miracle enough. He purred for the care, and growled because I had betrayed him, because he could no longer sleep indoors. Whenever he had come in lately, he'd piss everywhere, marking territory out of spite and jealousy. The following morning I gave him milk. He growled and purred, but when I petted him a little longer than usual, he only growled, as though to say, "What's with you, hypocrite, what are you doing that for? Don't tell me there's any space for love in this life. That's your human bullshit."

Of course, Stalin did not say this, at least not in so many words, but in many more growls. I did not argue.

Son of a Gun

B efore getting to know Sam, an Australian Blue Heeler, outside of Winnetoon, Nebraska, I used to take pride in belonging to the cat-loving rather than the dog-loving breed. In Croatia as a kid I had once thrown icy snowballs at a German shepherd, struck him on the muzzle, and he chased me, gaining on me; I jumped into a ten-foot hole. The dog growled at the edge of the pit for hours before he gave up. Frozen, I had barely managed to crawl out. That had confirmed my dislike of large dogs, and Sam did nothing to convert me, at first. I met him outside of my wife's uncle's farmhouse. Sam leaped at me, dug his thick and sharp claws into my belly, tearing my T-shirt and skin, and despite my anxiety and pain, I could see by his sloppy tongue that he grovelled for affection.

Jeanette's uncle Al offered us Sam to take care of. Al had moved into town and married a woman who hated dogs—not having animals around somehow proved to her that she was a city person. My tomcat Byeli and I were alarmed by the generous loan, but Jeanette thought it was an excellent idea, since we would live in a dilapidated farmhouse with lots of wildlife around us. And true enough, soon I appreciated his chasing away badgers and skunks.

I teased Sam with the Toyota siren; the pitch irritated his ears so that he'd lift his head straight up and howl, adjusting his pitch to merge with the car's. I tossed him antlers in the field, and he'd bring them back to me; I held them high, above my shoulder, and he'd leap and snatch them.

Despite Sam's treeing our cats, slurping calf dung, climbing the roof of our car and scratching it, pissing on our tires, tearing our clothes, and howling at three in the morning, I became fond of his shifty eyes, and of his waiting for us on the porch even when we were gone for days.

His previous caretaker, John, who lived alone in a cabin in the woods and occasionally helped out in the fields, claimed that Sam used to fetch newspapers from the mailbox every morning. I failed to get Sam to fetch my mail; my presence must have demolished his discipline. Sam was certainly a smart dog; as the only distinct variety of dog whose genes the American Kennel has not messed with, the Blue Heeler has retained wolfish vitality and cunning.

Though we had such a brave dog, I wanted a gun. All our neighbours had guns hanging in the backs of their pickups—if not because of coyotes, I wanted a gun because of the neighbours. My father-in-law, a full-time cowboy and ecology professor emeritus, carried a pistol—with a criss-crossed, engraved, wooden handle and a long barrel—in a little plastic case resembling a briefcase. On the morning of the first snow of the year, as the environmentalist, enshrouded in blue smoke, chainsawed trees to extend his pastures, I drove past him to borrow the gun at his house in the town of Center, population 120, six miles away. On the first curve I ran into the Holzer brothers. I waved and they waved, although our cars kept sliding. It was our point of honour—no matter what bind you were in, no matter how difficult it was to steer, you lifted one hand and waved. We may not have liked each other, we may have never talked to each other except about the precipitation and subsoil moisture, but here on the road we were a tight-knit community, good Cornhuskers. (Actually, we had talked several months before in a Creighton bar, beneath stuffed coyotes, horned owls and barn owls jutting forth from the wall. When I mentioned I had seen a horned owl, one brother said he'd shot two and, just the other day, he'd killed a barn owl in, of all places, his barn. To him that perhaps counted as a love of owls.) My topsy-turvy

Toyota Corona slid left and right, but steadied itself like a pair of skis.

On another downhill curve, the mailman's car showed up. Greedy for job offers and good news from Croatia (although only bad ones were coming with shelling and towns on fire), I braked. He'd be happy he didn't have to take the long detour to our mailbox. He should have been smiling at the thought, but was he smiling? My car swerved, and it didn't slow down. Would I smash into him, kill both of us? My car spun, straightened out, but dragged along a ditch and dipped into sumac brush. The mailman stopped gracefully, grinned out the window, and said, "Braking downhill in snow, a useless proposition. You want a ride to the old Becker place? He's got a four-wheeler."

"No, thanks, I'll walk."

"Are you sure?"

But soon Becker showed up in his old beat-up pickup and gave me a ride to the car. "Did the mailman tell you I got stranded?" I asked.

"No, I saw how fast you were going and I heard noises, so I said, what the heck, I might as well help." With his engine idling next to my ditched car, he talked. "You young people ought to be ashamed of yourselves. My generation, we built all the roads and most of the rails, and you can't even repair them!"

He could have said we could not even drive on them decently, but he did not, though he did ask, "Do you pay taxes?" I hesitated with the answer, wishing I made enough money to pay taxes, and nodded slightly, ambiguously, taking the question to be merely a rhetorical introduction to one of his points, which I guess it was.

"If we all honestly paid taxes, we'd have more than enough, no three-trillion-dollar deficits, for sure. We'd be able to rebuild the roads, send men to Mars, keep everybody health-insured, but because everybody's a cheat, we can't do that. When I was a young man, I paid all my taxes, and I went to Lincoln to see whether our honourable community members did their share. I found out that many rich farmers cheated, and I, a poor dumb farmer, didn't. So I said, I'll show you who's dumb. I visited the state treasurer, but he wouldn't let me examine his records, so I went to the governor, and by golly, pretty soon I had them all back to back! Even the governor was embarrassed!"

The old man roped my bumper while his little mutt barked at me with genuine animosity, perhaps smelling Sam's urine, and pulled out the car. When I drove back, I saw that the mailman had left something in my box—he had not bothered to deliver it to me while I was in the ditch. Junk mail, bills, and a package. Musical Heritage Society sent us more tapes because I had not cancelled the membership on time. I thought I would mail the tapes back, but I tore the package to peep in. Beethoven's five piano concertos. As soon as I shook the snow off my work shoes, I stuck a tape in the stereo and listened to the prolonged wistful variations of a quiet piano, which filled me with grandiose gloom as though it was I who had experienced all the inspiration. But amidst the great sadness I absorbed from Beethoven, I experienced the small sadness of not having managed to get the gun, that somehow I was doomed to be gunless.

I walked out on the tilting porch and shouted for Sam to come back—in the white fields with yellow stubble, the Blue Heeler was chasing Anguses; Al certainly wouldn't have allowed him to do that. Sam came back, leaped at me, which in the winter I did not mind; his claws did not reach me through my thick sweater. I scratched his neck, pulled his blue-grey hair that resembled small porcupine quills, and thought about how Sam would not be so ornery if he weren't so alone.

To assuage his loneliness, we got two puppies, one male, one female. In the reprieve from the cold, Sam played with the young

103

Dobermans. The boy had huge paws and promised to become larger than Sam. As the two tumbled across the yard, Sam must have appreciated that prospect, for soon he led the pup farther and farther into the hills, and after one such escapade, the pup did not return. The coyotes probably ate him. Sam feigned some sadness, blinking cleverly. His body hunched as though he were depressed or as if he expected a blow, but he did not keep up the act for long. Now the true game started, with the female pup. He rolled and tumbled with her, got carrot-like erections, rubbed against her back, but did not enter her, at least not with me around.

The pup grew so fast that she too would soon be larger than Sam, and rather than "fix" her and have two dogs to feed, I gave her to Dave, a community-college student, along with forty dollars for dog food. Forty dollars of booze later, that same evening, Dave got nabbed for drunk driving, was sent to the regional jail, got into a fight, and plucked a man's eye out of its socket with his fingers. When I heard that, I despaired: you give away a sweet pup, and pretty soon, somebody's eye is torn out.

Sam pined away for his vivacious jailbait. But, as soon as Holzer's young beagle showed up (the Holzers came over to cut some wood, Al's present to them) Sam cheered up and rolled in the grass with her; they bit at each other's ears and licked foreheads, howled, rushed through crumbling barns, hunted possum, and when she faltered from exhaustion, with her tongue on a shoe, Sam mounted her tenderly, his tongue on her nape. Even three weeks later, Sam and the beagle kept tumbling, rolling across the yard among the tumbleweeds—driven by dusty winds—that accumulated on the fence before the cow watering drum. Who knows how long their intimacy would have lasted—but Holzer, who did not like a dog who would not stay close to home, shot and killed her.

Now Sam ran around looking for her, and after two days, he could barely open his bloodshot eyes.

After that he grew even more viciously lonely. When Jeanette's young niece and her friends visited, he gazed into their eyes with his tongue sentimentally loose, licked their cheeks, and they hugged him. Because he yearned for company so much, he was no guard dog. If a total stranger with a gun showed up—sometimes Al allowed pheasant and deer hunters on the land—he'd leap and grovel for joy. Whenever Jeanette and I took walks, he followed us in the fields. For Jeanette and me, it was a little awkward to cross wire fences, press the topmost one, step on tiptoe and lift one leg over the wires, or crawl beneath or between them. Sam simply jumped the fence.

In the field we once found a stillborn calf, with gaping bloody red holes in the black fur. Sam took quite a few big bites out of the carcass, and when he was done he pissed around it, reserving it for later, though this was not his territory, but coyote land. Only when we walked him could he go this far away from the house and eat carcasses. He could take the road to villages six miles away, in either direction; there, the coyotes could not stop him. But here in the field, he had to yield.

Rather than managing to expand his territory by marking further afield, Sam lost it. Every night coyotes seemed to come closer and closer to the house, so that Sam was circumscribed to an area of three to four acres, and during the day double that, but still mostly outside of the range of dead calves (each spring there were at least three stillbirths).

Coyotes came so close that they dug a nest beneath our defunct Chevy pickup in the pasture. One sunny noon a mother with half a dozen pups as yellow as the dry prairie grass peeped out from beneath the shelter. Rusty, tilting, the pickup merged with the landscape, for what is iron but a sort of stone, and what is landscape but stone with a bit of green and yellow life cracking through it? Almost every round hill had an old stripped pickup growing yellow among bones of abandoned cows now blazingly white. To my mind, pickup bodies weren't junk at all. To coyotes' minds, far from junk, they became homes.

Once, before having a cup of coffee, I looked out the window and saw half a dozen cats in trees. "Look," I said to Jeanette, "even our small kittens love to climb trees." She interrupted proofreading her essay on *Paradise Regained*—she studied for an English degree across the Missouri River, in Vermillion—and pointed out a detail which I had missed: Sam. I went out and shouted at him, trying to sound as forbidding as possible. Sam rolled on the ground, contritely, and looked at me sideways. Often if he had done something wrong, like chewed my wool sweater or eaten my shoe, even before I knew it, because he must have assumed I did know it, he'd coil on his back with his paws in the air, as though to defend himself. The difference now was that as I kept shouting at him, he looked slyly at me, one of his eyes closing and opening, winking—as though to say, You look pretty when you're angry! I told him to go away, pointing to a barn, and he went there, looking from a distance as I collected the precariously perched kitties and let them into the house, where Sam was allowed only if temperatures dipped below zero. Before us, he'd had to weather minus twenties. The first time we invited him inside, he would not enter the house, as though crossing the doorstep was a grave violation of human and canine laws. And in rural Nebraska, it was. Once, after Sam had jumped on a kitchen table, Jeanette's uncle—not Al but his older brother Jim—had beaten Sam with a tractor chain. Clearly remembering the punishment, Sam would not enter our house, and even as I pulled him in, he squealed. Soon, however, he got used to being inside; in the morning, rather than squeal to be let out, he stood in the kitty litter box, his back feet in the sand, front outside, aiming precisely at the middle of the box. And then he covered his crap, while cats, in utter alarm, watched from cupboards and bookshelves.

In sub-zero temperatures it seemed that Sam was simply too old—seven or eight, nobody knew precisely—to take the weather, although local ranchers would have deliberately made him stay outdoors, as they did with their dogs and cows. Old barns that used to protect cows now fell apart, some dismembered for lumber or new pasture, and the cows huddled together in biting wind chills.

Sometimes Sam left us for several days because he participated in "cattle drives." Local cattle farmers, in boots and cowboy hats, rode horses and bullied cattle, moving them to winter pastures with corn stubble in a festival of manhood. Women were not welcome—neither were city slickers, like myself—to the chagrin of Jeanette, who, although an excellent and experienced rider, was allowed to join only once, to take pictures of the cowboys. Sam thrived then, living up to his reputation as a Heeler—he ran after straying cows in an outside loop so that they would return to the herd. He could not do that with bulls, but on the other hand, bulls always stayed in the same pastures.

While Sam was away, I missed him, particularly when I went into the basement to throw logs into the furnace, because now, without the canine, possums and badgers began to return. I walked down the wooden steps with a long poker in my hands, so that if one of those creatures startled me, I could chase it away, which I did by banging a big metal sheet rolled upright in a spiral (I thought I would use it to repair a furnace duct, but never got around to doing it). At the metallic bang, possums ambled away slowly in the dark. Basement light bulbs quickly burnt out because the high mineral content of the water from our leaky pipes corroded the wiring that sent waves of stray voltage, so that our cats, when we wanted to pet them, jumped away before fire would leap crookedly from our fingertips. I felt ashamed of being uncomfortable in the dark basement, listening to the sounds of meek wildlife, with faces of badgers, bull snakes and foxes merging surreally in my imagination into an infernal painting by Bosch. But rabies was a good excuse for the discomfort. So, although we grew used to a baby skunk who ate cat food on the porch without stinking up the place, we beheld Sam joyously.

For a couple of days Sam ran, threatened, and even killed the sampling of prairie wildlife, until my going downstairs to light a fire became a delightfully earthy rite: I'd toss in some ash and red hardwood, after chopping stray branches and edges of thick logs to fit into the large mouth past its thick iron lip, a door with the name of Marshaltown, Iowa, bulging in cast iron. Orange fire in my eyes, smoke in my nostrils, and tar on my fingers gave me many sensations. Among them, I was loading the steam engine of a train and crossing the continent, and what a luxurious train it appeared when I climbed out to face a briskly black firmament, a frosty Milky Way, coyotes howling, and among them, Sam's barking. Some dogs did seem to be a cross between coyote and dog. The Holzers' mutt, with his thick orange fur and narrow muzzle, looked like a coyote.

Several nights after Sam came back from the cattle drives, we certainly appreciated him. Sam growled, with his back to our window. The light from the window usually reassured him, but not enough that night—he moaned and squealed when he did not pant or bark.

"I wish we had a gun," I said. "If there's a pack of rabid coyotes there, I could scare them. Poor Sam has to do all the work himself."

"Do rabid coyotes get scared?" Jeanette asked.

Sam, perhaps tired of fear, ran into a grove in our yard. Late at night we heard bulls hollering and somewhere a cow screamed as though a beast were slaughtering her.

"Something big out there," Jeanette said.

In the morning we forgot about the incident, but in the afternoon, as I hadn't seen Sam, I wondered about him. I was taking a crap in the grove, aiming at the hole of the previous outhouse site, because a crew of wasps now occupied our outhouse and they had already stung me four times. Standing up from my innocuous way of dealing with nature, I noticed Sam, not far off, watching me, a plea in his eyes. A red stripe went straight from his neck down his chest on one side, and a dark stripe on another.

I scrutinized the stripes. A short while later, I asked Jeanette, "Have you seen Sam lately?"

She bent down and checked his fur. "It's blood, isn't it?"

"Boy, that's strange," I commented. "Sam is so fast, I can't see how another dog would get him."

"Coyotes may have ganged up on him."

"Or could it be a bobcat?"

"Oh, I forgot to tell you, there's been a cougar around. The Holzers have seen it, and so have the Kruppels, near Winnetoon. I bet it's the cougar."

"Come on, he wouldn't survive that, would he?"

"The cougar must have had him by the neck, see the big marks?"

"What a brave dog! He probably attacked the cougar!"

"I am going to town to ask my brother about the cougar reports."

"Ask him to finally give you a gun."

She was gone.

Faithful Sam: he was always there, guarding us, and we didn't even feed him much except for his dry food. True, lately he'd been piling rabbits and squirrels in the yard, letting them rot—his version of cooking. I went to the fridge and gave him a piece of a dead cow, which he devoured in two gulps and growled. "Sure thing," I said. "You understand the importance of iron in your blood. Here, have some more." I was heartened. Sam would recover.

So now, while Jeanette was away, I tried to examine Sam's wounds, but he ducked. I didn't insist because I could hurt him. He stood and walked with a surprising amount of strength. I admired what a broad genetic pool could do for your stamina.

Soon Tim and Jeanette were back. Tim called Sam, Sam jumped at him, gave him a lick on his chin below his cigarette. Tim pulled Sam by the neck, right by the wound. (I resented that bit of cowboy machismo—Tim played rough and independent, and yet, though he was twenty-eight, he stayed at his parents' place and constantly begged for loans.) Sam didn't squirm; a little stump of a tail, cut by his first owner because of a peculiar tail-hating aesthetic, continued to wag.

"Oh, my God," shouted Tim. "That's not blood. It's shit! It's shit!" His voice grew shrill.

"It can't be," I said. "Look at how red it is."

Jeanette smelled it and said, "No, it's blood. Old blood smells like this."

"Like shit? You are crazy," Tim said.

"I worked in a hospital, you haven't. This is old stinky blood."

"You two are crazy, man!"

"You are crazy," I said. "Have you brought us a gun? You know, here without a neighbour within a mile radius, we need it."

"I'll bring you a pistol. It's louder, if you want to scare coyotes, cougars and shit." Now he went through Sam's wounds again. "It's shit. At least I can tell shit. Yuck."

"Come on, it's a wound."

"There's no wound crust, no scratch, nothing deep in the hairs!" His fingers groped through the hairs.

"It was a tooth that pierced just in one spot," I said.

"What's wrong with the two of you?"

"We are sorry to see the romance go: our dog fighting a cougar," Jeanette said.

"Sick," he commented.

I grew impatient with Sam's being insulted like that, so I examined the wounds. I smelled my fingers. "Shit, it is shit!"

Tim was about to leave.

"You know, Tim," I said, "the worst thing about this is that I think the shit is mine." I put warmth into my voice, confiding.

"How disgusting!" Tim squealed.

"I was joking. I don't think he would have gone into the outhouse, but then, again . . ."

Tim was in the car and down the lane.

"That was the last time he'll come here," Jeanette said.

"He'll be back before long to bum two bucks for cigarettes."

Our brave dog cowered away, inexpressible sadness in his eyes, perhaps for the loss of glory. At least he got a steak, and now I understood why he was reluctant to have his wounds examined. But he kept the stripes—they probably worked as a kind of diplomatic passport that allowed him to cross into the coyote land with the aura of human prestige and immunity.

The following morning, pretty early, I stole my wife's slippers and went into the yard. "Where are you going?"

"I am going out to free the cougars. They've been caged for too long."

I freed the cougars in the outhouse and when I stood up, I stood like a monkey, pretty low, so the wasps from the nest on the roof wouldn't swoop down to sting me.

Sam squealed and jubilantly ran out of the yard and into the woods near a narrow creek among cottonwoods, where ordinarily he would not dare run during the day.

It was July 4th, the one event that excited Knox County. A Desert Storm war hero delivered speeches amidst fireworks and flags. Later his wife was found in bed with her skull smashed. She'd had several lovers while he had been in the desert and then finally left him. Before police could question the hero, he drove into a field, put a gun barrel below his chin, and pulled the trigger. The trouble was he did not seem to know where the vital part of the brain was. He blew off his chin, his tongue, his nose, his eyes, and the frontal lobes of his brain, but he stayed alive, despite blood clogging his throat and filling his lungs. After that, I did not desire a rifle that bad.

Just when we began to treat Sam as a great pal—we now combed his hair with a rough brush and bought medicine for his lingering eye infection (one eye seemed constantly bloodshot)—we had to leave. Our time of poverty seemed to be up. I got a job offer at a university in Minnesota. In two years we had made hardly any friends in the area; it seemed like it would take fifty years to begin to fit in. We dropped a tomcat off behind a cheeseburger joint. This may sound cruel, but a month before, we had picked him up as a stray in Center because his ears were torn, and we bought cream for him and nursed him back to good health, and then, as we packed our car, he snuck into the house, and in a couple of seconds killed two kittens, biting through their necks, and wounded the third, before we noticed and kicked him out. When we dropped him off, he was better off than he had been before. We gave away some cats to Jeanette's relatives; others, we had advertised in the local papers and then we left sacks of food atop the furnace for the toms who had not shown up. We asked Jeanette's brother and her father and uncles to take care of Sam. With heavy hearts and a couple of dearest cats, we drove away from our muddy driveway.

Three months later, when we came for a visit, there were no cats and no Sam. Skunks had moved under our porch, droves of bickering badgers and raccoons into the barns, and old possums, who looked like ancient balding professors, into the basement. I started a reluctant, heavy, smoky and stinky fire, which smoked us out of the house. We found out that nobody would have Sam; people feared that he would bark and urinate too much, scratch up car roofs, bite through ropes, eat shoes, and he would not stay on a chain. Al, his owner, had died of a stroke. In his will he did not mention Sam. So, Sam kept visiting the Holzers, who could not stand a dog that left too much, and now apparently, a dog that stayed too much. Holzer killed Sam with a hunting rifle, and dumped his body in the ravine nearby, which was also his garbage dump.

Tumbling: Maine

My son and I visited Stephen, my friend who ran an art colony on an island in Maine. We drove down the lane to his refurbished red farmhouse. His home had huge floor tiles, each one about four square feet, a bit uneven, thick, foot-worn to a polish. They reminded me of churches in Europe.

"Stephen, these tiles are impressive," I said.

"They better be," he said. "I bought a whole damned monastery in France to get these tiles."

"Really? You're crazy."

"I had the monastery floor taken apart and shipped to me. I still have a lot of stone I'll use somehow."

"How did you find the monastery?"

"On eBay."

"You could have just as well bought hundreds of bottles of Bordeaux."

"I could have, but these tiles are more solid. By the way, it's fantastic to see you," he said. "Let's have some special wine for the occasion. You know, I have this wine cellar that I inherited from one of my friends, a large brewing company heir, who died in Munich. He left millions to his various wives and lovers, and I was the executor of his will, and he left me just three hundred bottles of damned fine French wines, which are probably past their prime, but each one goes for minimum five hundred bucks. I haven't had any yet. Would you mind splitting a bottle?"

"Yes, I would mind," I said with the ironic intonation. "Why didn't he drink them up before he died?"

"He was a sick man, an alcoholic. Strange karma, isn't it, for a beer mogul. He could drink only vodka or gin, pure. He needed an immediate alcoholic surge. Wine was too slow for him. The heritage of wine was wasted on him. After his death, his autopsy showed that his brain had shrunk to the size of an average apple."

"Okay, let's not think about apples," I said, "but grapes, and let's drink. The drive was hell."

So we drank a bottle, and it was all right. I forgot its name. Maybe we should have decanted it. Then we drank a bottle of wine I got from a friend of mine, a wine distributor, an Englishman—a Californian merlot that would sell in the range of forty or so, and it was much tastier than the somehow dusty and sour old French wine. My son played the cello, a Chopin piece, soulfully, and I wondered why he abused himself so to become a virtuoso. He reminded me of the anecdote from Diogenes Laertius, which goes approximately like this—Diogenes listened to a young man play the lyre, and the more he played, the sadder Diogenes was, and he started weeping. What's wrong, the host said, Doesn't he play beautifully? Yes, he does. The more he plays, the more I realize how much time the poor lad has spent practicing. I mourn for all that time he wasted. I felt a bit like that for my son, but then I thought, maybe the fucking French wine was making me sentimental and irrational.

Next time I visited Stephen, I said, "How is your cellar holding up?"

"Better than it should," he replied.

"How so?"

"I forgot the code and my wife is hiding it from me. She wants me to quit drinking. So I have kind of quit. And also, she doesn't understand that wine is not like a museum. Wine improves for a while and then gets worse, and museums get better and better with age. We should drink it all for a month and have a festival of silliness but instead it will be really corked and foul. But what do I care?

I can just imagine how the wine is doing in a vault. It's like Italian liras after the introduction of the euro. They were still good for a year and you could exchange them, and now, they are just pretty things to put on the wall. And not even all that pretty. The French francs are prettier and so are the Dutch guilders. But they are all now worthless."

Zidane the Ram

To have a happy childhood, you need to have a warm and furry pet—that seems to be a universally acknowledged principle. My daughter Eva wanted to have a very furry pet, and she's had and loved cats. I wouldn't get her a real bear; teddy bears didn't work for her, and so she created a friend for herself, a little black bear. It was an imaginary bear, and the friendship with him lasted even beyond the time my wife and I imagined she was through with it.

While Eva was sociable with her friends and cats, she relied on Little Black Bear, who was her most intimate companion, always at her side, keeping her warm and protected. We lived in Shawnee State Forest, in Ohio. One day Eva decided she needed to meet her friend. She put on her yellow rubber boots and walked out into the yard, past the old tobacco barn, and then up Snake Hill. We called it Snake Hill because Jeanette had once stepped on a rattlesnake there. She wasn't bitten, but she was terrified enough that she didn't like to hike there. Eva walked up the cleared path along a flash-flood ravine. I followed her, to see how far this three-year-old girl would dare to walk into the dark forest. I don't think she was aware of me walking some hundred paces behind her. She crested the hill and kept going. She was going faster and faster. Afraid of losing her in the bushes, I accelerated, and caught her by the scruff of the neck, her coat. She shouted, "Let me go!"

"What are you doing? Running away from home?"

"I am going to see Little Black Bear."

"There are no bears in our forest."

"Yes, there are. I must see him."

I put her on my shoulders, astride my neck. She kicked, and I held on to her boots, but she managed to slip out of the grip and banged me with the heel right on the nose. Luckily, it was a rubber sole, but my nose hurt to the point of stargazing. I brought her home and she wept for half an hour because her meeting with Little Black Bear was foiled.

Although she thought she had disappointed her friend, Little Black Bear continued to be her trusted buddy. He could help her in crisis. When she was five years old, Jeanette and she visited a music store with all sorts of toys for kids. Eva took an exotic red frog (made out of plastic) and put it in her jacket. The shopkeeper noticed that, and said, "Your child is shoplifting!"

"Why did you steal the frog?" Jeanette asked.

"I didn't do it. Little Black Bear did. He put it in my pocket."

Jeanette returned the frog to the shop assistant, and the disgraced half of the family left the shop. So when Eva wanted to learn to play the guitar, and I suggested taking cheap lessons at that store, Jeanette told me this anecdote to explain why they couldn't go back. "But after three years, he wouldn't recognize you, and why would he care?"

We moved to Pennsylvania, to a forested hill. One night, after Jeanette had treated our deck, I took the back-door exit to go to my studio. There was a loud cracking of branches a couple of yards in front of me. What was that? Where was my German shepherd? I walked in and turned on the light, and there was someone or something cowering in the doghouse. "It must be a bear," I said.

"Really," Eva said.

"Yes, I think it's a Big Black Bear."

"I hope I see him."

"Who knows, maybe it's the Little Black Bear who has become the Big Black Bear, and he came to see you."

Eva's eyes grew wide—clearly, she was tempted to believe this, although she no longer believed in the Easter Bunny, having caught me hiding the eggs in the bushes around the house.

The following day a fifty-pound bag of dog food disappeared. I found it half-eaten way out in the woods. Clearly, a raccoon couldn't do that, although raccoons can hardly ever be underestimated. Must've been a bear.

Then, as we had a pot roast in the oven, there was rumbling. I went outside. The bear had put his paws through the ventilation opening in the wall and torn out the insulation.

Next day I saw him in the bushes, not twenty yards away. The sun was lighting the green of the bushes and the trees, and amidst the green stood this awesome shiny black bear. I stood there and so did he. I wondered what he thought. Slowly he turned away and ambled and then ran, producing much branch cracking. I was glad I hadn't stumbled into him.

He also dug holes in the garden soil. Maybe he didn't do it, but now I blamed him for every incidence of damage in the vicinity. I called the game warden, and asked him what to do about the bear. He came up the hill and said there were so many bears that they ran out of cages.

"Generally," he said, "we trap them and then take them to a state forest 100 miles away. Sometimes they make it back; most often they stay."

"If he bothers us again, can we get a friend to shoot him?"

"No, that's illegal, other than during hunting season."

"I don't want to wait for the hunting season." I showed him the damage the bear had done to the house and the garden. "Can't I shoot him to protect my property and children?"

"Well, nobody could prevent you from self-defence," he said.

Anyway, I went to Dick's Sporting Goods, and asked for a gun that would be good enough to kill a bear, but I decided against buying one. Instead I bought a .22 Remington to shoot raccoons who ate my chickens.

As though understanding all these conversations, the bear didn't show up again. Maybe someone else shot him. Maybe he was trapped. But Eva was certainly sad that she didn't get to see him. I imagine that she did think that it was Little Black Bear, who tried to visit her as Big Black Bear. Just as she was prevented by me from visiting him in her toddlerhood, he was prevented from visiting her now by mean men, including her dad.

But I was not all that mean. I wanted her to have a happy childhood and she was already ten, running out of childhood. Jeanette agreed that a sheep might do for happiness. But not one; two, a male and a female.

"This is not Noah's ark," I said.

The two lambs came out of the Toyota Corolla and hopped in the yard. The short-haired female was white and Eva named her Leche. The black male was smaller and limped. Eva named him Café. Leche ran away from us but Café liked to be scratched on the head, and he looked at me with his wet eyes and snorted. He was two months older than Leche and no longer needed milk—he was happy with grass and cracked corn. Jeanette bought him for ten dollars, as he was trampled by the flock and the farmer didn't think he would make a good ram. Leche cost thirty dollars. She clamoured for milk, and Jeanette bought her formula. The milk had to be thicker than cow milk, richer in protein. So twice a day Leche sucked milk out of a plastic bottle, a quart each time. Yet if you stroked her, she would leap away from you and then come back. She tugged downward at the bottle nipple. We had a chicken coop without chickens so we put the lambs in it, elevated from the ground.

Although Leche got a lot of milk, Café grew faster and pretty soon he was larger than her and his limp was gone. He ran around the green hopping and galloping. The German shepherd loved the sheep. It seemed a natural friendship. Jude teased Café and Café ran after him and tried to butt the dog.

It seemed he was growing horns but he tended to rub his head against the trees, and so his bumps didn't grow. Maybe his sort would grow horns in the fields without trees to rub against. Because of his butting tendencies I renamed him Zidane, after the amazing French-Algerian soccer star, who blew away a world championship for France with a red-card-yielding head-butt. Maybe that was an unfortunate name as my ram grew to butt more and more, banging against the house door at night; he became a butt-head. When Leche was weaned from milk, and they got cracked corn to eat, he would butt her away and eat first. Nevertheless, she followed him everywhere and they roamed pretty widely, like a pair of wild dogs, even to the neighbour's corn field. Since they raided the garden, eating young cabbage, peppers, and strawberries, I had to build a fence all around the garden, mostly because of the sheep and perhaps the deer. Now their task was to test the fence and crawl under it whenever possible. I'd have to corner them and catch them and lift them over the fence into the yard. They were a lot of work for pets, but the only pet was Zidane. You could scratch his head and he'd rub against your thighs. He smelled like a big old wool sweater. His head stayed black but his body turned light chocolate brown. His hairs were long and curly, and he was a beautiful tall ram with huge balls. To get corn from me he attacked the garage where I stored it. He banged against the doors, sometimes as early as four in the morning. *Mehr, mehr.* I joked that he could speak German, as that sounded like "more, more" in German. And when I looked up the etymology of Zidane, this came up: *The term "Zidan" or "Zaydaan" is derived from the Arabic root word of "Zeed" which simply means "more" . . . thus the term or name "Zidan" would mean "a lot more."* I don't know whether all rams are quite that lusty or whether, because of growing up with a handicap, he compensated with his huge appetite.

For the hell of it, I sometimes went down on all fours to head-butt with Zidane but his skull was too hard for me; plus, as I'd had a concussion ten years ago, I didn't think it was good to shake up the soup in my skull. As a kid I used to have a sheep, and no doubt it was a ram. We spent hours head-butting. He'd dig his hooves in the ground and charge at full speed straight into my skull, knocking me over. It hurt, but to be a good sport I persevered. He also ate all the roses and I climbed cherry trees and tore branches off so he could enjoy the leaves. My mother didn't appreciate the sheer devastation Shestica inflicted, and one day, while I was being a good boy and attending a Baptist conference in a village ten kilometres away—I had biked to it and worked on my salvation, enjoying all the imagery of sheep in the church—Mother sold the sheep. On the way back from the conference, I passed by the corner tavern at the end of our block. There was a sign, *Svjeza janjetina*. Fresh lamb. I panicked. I didn't have any reason to think my pet was being eaten by the fat, ruddy-cheeked drunks in blue workers' uniforms. Yet my sheep was gone, and clearly, it was my pet that was eaten on the spot. I learned that having pets was a sorrowful affair, almost as sorrowful as having a dead father, who'd died in front of me when I was eleven.

Zidane loved to be scratched on the head, and he spent hours rubbing his head against trees.

Leche and Zidane raided our garden, eating broccoli, cabbage, and they did not know that it was a moral issue. I'd run into the garden and shout at them to leave the fenced area but the garden was too large, and it was usually an athletic event of running around, picking up a stick and threatening to whack them. Some of them I broke on Zidane's forehead, and it never seemed to hurt him. Rather it stimulated him. He'd angle his head and look at me challengingly.

Usually I'd have to grab him by the collar and drag him out of the garden. He liked to hang around me and if I hiked in the woods he'd follow like a dog. A friend of mine, a writer named Jeff Parker, visited me and commented that sheep were a lot like dogs, only dumber. I actually didn't like their intelligence to be insulted. They were smart for what they wanted. In general, it seems to me when we judge the intelligence of other creatures who have other frames of reference, that it's hard to judge them fairly.

Zidane rubbed against everything—cars, deck, trees—when he wanted to be shorn. We wanted to call in a shearer but somehow never got around to it. I used a large pair of scissors and tried my best to get rid of his wool but it was too thick. It harboured little creatures, and he was like the angel in *A Very Old Man with Enormous Wings*, with his hairs strewn with parasites, which was actually a very endearing and sociable trait. When he stood and cogitated and ruminated, looking at the humans around him at a distance, our chickens would jump on his back, sometime three at a time, and peck at him. I wish I had taken a picture of it, but all I did was admire the symbiosis of three species, or maybe four or five, but three that I could immediately identify. Our eggs were the best ever—everybody who ate them said so—and they were a result of free-range rummaging in the woods, and fields, and exercise which consisted of dodging hawks which sometimes descended like bombs from the thermals and the tall oaks, straight at the chickens. The chickens were eating worms in the woods, eating grass in the field, oyster shells which we gave them for calcium, and jumping on sheep and eating parasites. Maybe this was the ingredient which gave special spice to the eggs. Of course, the fact that they discovered a dead deer, and that they ate the deer (why call deer "venison"?), pecking at it like vultures, that could not be neglected. Zidane didn't mind the chickens but if we gave them corn, he chased them. While one set was being intimidated, another came from behind and pecked more corn. In the end he just stood and marvelled at how he could do nothing to save the food for himself. If we fed him and Leche only, he'd mercilessly push her and butt her so he got most of the grains. It seemed it would be best for them to eat only grass and hay and tree leaves, but they were pets after all, and it's like having kids. You know candy is no good for them, that you should instead offer spinach, but you still occasionally, for birthdays and Halloween, give them horrifying candy. Grains were bound to be better. I even got them oats. But feeding them too well made Zidane terribly sick, and he hid under the chicken coop, and bloated up to twice his normal size, and he panted, his black and purple tongue hanging out the side of his mouth. He gurgled, and I thought he was breathing his last.

"Look what you've done," Jeanette said. "You killed poor Zidane by feeding him grains. I told you to stop it."

"I didn't know."

"You're a murderer," she said, and called the vet.

"I didn't know you liked him."

"I didn't know either, but I feel sorry for him. Now I see I do."

The vet took him into the clinic, gave him B vitamins and some other shots, even a transfusion, and Zidane came back, like new, and wanted more grains, but for a while he'd get only grass and hay. His salvation cost me $500, but I was happy, and I petted him and scratched his hard head, and he bobbed his head up and down. I guess he must have had some kind of natural psalm in his head, praising the Lord for life, something like Psalm 23.

1 The Lord is my shepherd; I shall not want. 2 He maketh me to lie down in green pastures: he leadeth me beside the still waters. 3 He restoreth my soul: he leadeth me in the paths of righteousness for his name's sake. 4 Yea, though I walk through the valley of the shadow of death, I will fear no evil: for thou art

*with me; thy rod and thy staff they comfort me. 5 Thou preparest
a table before me in the presence of mine enemies: thou anoint-
est my head with oil; my cup runneth over. 6 Surely goodness and
mercy shall follow me all the days of my life: and I will dwell in
the house of the LORD for ever.*

Maybe King David would have been a better name for him?

Zidane smelled wonderful, like an Icelandic sweater. He followed our cars and Leche followed him, and so they galloped half
a mile down the mountain on which we lived. It was really a hill,
eroded by millennia of winds and rains and ice, but historically
it was a god-installed mountain, one of the oldest in the world,
with the euphonious name, Bald Eagle Mountain. It stretches for
50 miles in Central Pennsylvania, the last ridge of the Appalachians
facing the Alleghenies over a wide valley, just over the crest of the
hill from us, at some 2,000 feet. It was a major fault line with the
tectonic plates of Pangaea, Europe and the Americas dividing right
here, but one part of Europe drifted and got stuck to America, while
a new line was formed and split with the ocean. I know little of
geology but this would make sense, to indicate why the Northeast
is so inherently snobbish and standoffish with the rest of America.
From this prehistoric ridge, Zidane would run into the first valley
of the Appalachian range, probably not worrying about geology at
all, his hoofs raising a cloud of dust. And he'd go back up. On one
occasion the sheep disappeared and were gone for two days. I don't
know where the hell they went, but I looked for them with our German shepherd, Jude, all over the place, up the ridge, down to the
valley, east and west, and I shouted to no avail.

And at night, if I slept in my studio, he would butt loudly
against the door of the garage above which my studio sat. In the
morning there were grease marks and dark stripes left on the white
of the door. He would have loved to just stay indoors with us, to be

our pet, but with his enormously productive digestive system, that would have been disgusting.

He grew to consider himself the master of the hill. I am not sure what all his nights were like but with bears occasionally visiting, I wondered what it took to keep them away. Our dog, Jude, would sometimes stay indoors most cleverly when he could smell bear.

Zidane attacked my son once when Joseph wasn't watching and knocked him to the ground. Joseph limped for a few days but was all right. He knocked down Eva and terrified Shara, her Indian friend, who no longer liked to visit. Sure, sometimes I limited the sheep to the lower field and spent five hundred bucks building a long fence with my friend Boris. They could be contained in the field but they hated it. Soon they were out of food, and giving them hay in the middle of the summer made no sense. We had plenty of grass, and I bought a scythe, thinking I would harvest it, but I never got to it. Of course, I should have, it would have been a very useful exercise, beautiful in many ways. Especially with the snakes around, which we had—copperheads and rattlesnakes.

Once Zidane knocked down Jeanette, and she said she wished she hadn't saved his life. He got me a couple of times but it never hurt all that much. However, one time when I was planting an arbour vitae, I stood up and suddenly I saw Zidane flying at me. It was too late to react. He connected with my right shin right below the knee. The pain was instant and intense. I wrestled him to the ground, and knelt on his throat. His thick grey-black tongue popped out and he made a choking noise. I let go, but I was mad. Did he break my leg? He certainly bruised the bone, and I suspect he may have cracked it as the shin was blue for two weeks, and the pain persisted for two months. Now I was more cautious with him and if he reared his hind hooves to get leverage in order to start at me, I either evaded him behind a tree, or wrestled him, which he may have liked as a buddy kind of thing. Sometimes, when I had less patience, I whacked him on the head with a snow shovel. That seemed to tickle him.

So, what to do?

His balls hung low, and they were enormous—big enough for an elephant. Clearly, he had way too much testosterone, yet, strangely enough, after two years, he still had not become a father. He had tried, but somehow always on the wrong occasion. Once, during an ice storm, on a slope, he climbed Leche. She didn't mind—she had angled herself seductively. Each time he was over her, with his two hooves on the ice, he slid and fell, and slid down the hill, banging against the house. He stood up, climbed up the hill, tried again, and slid again. I pulled her down the hill on flat terrain, so he'd be able to procreate, but since I touched her, he grew jealous and furious, as though I had wanted to do it. He ran at me to crush me and I evaded him, and he slid on ice way down the hill. And when he came back up, he tried to get me again. Now it was more important for him to get rid of male competition, it seemed, and he forgot about sex. Aggression seemed more intoxicating in his testosterone cloud. Despite his impressive balls, he may have been sterile, or Leche infertile. For a while I had wanted little lambs—they are such charming creatures—but now I was glad we had none. Of course, a real farmer would have had lots of them, and would have enjoyed the organic dishes made from them.

Meanwhile, friends of mine and I were discussing whole foods at Otto's brewery: you either didn't eat meat or you did. If you did, you either killed it yourself, or delegated it to others, which certainly was no better but in a way worse. And you either ate concentration-camp food, miserable chickens locked up and tortured with antibiotics and light and shit, or you ate free range. If free range, then, probably from small quantities, and in small quantities, it meant you would actually know the meat you were eating. In other words, each small-time farmer, especially European-style, eats his pets. The shepherd grows a few head of sheep and cows, and then kills his pets. That must be an extremely painful moment for him but, at the same time, a real moment. You kill a bit of yourself, of your love, your beautiful world, in order to eat, and a feast is a double kind of thing—it's always a funeral.

If Zidane gave me trouble, shouldn't I just eat him? To begin with, why raise sheep? Should they not support me after I've supported them and fed them for so long? They enjoy a couple of good years of fantastically free life, and then we have a feast and enjoy them and also feel sad for them. Yes, that made perfect sense. Who is serving whom? Am I their pet, or are they my pet? Now, these are simplistic questions, which in a brewery may sound deep, and in some way, are. I decided I could not eat Zidane, but that it would be better for my friends to eat him rather than to sue me for broken legs, as Zidane was becoming more and more aggressive. And what about Leche? She seemed to be so dependent on Zidane that it would make most sense to let her become food as well.

Moreover, we were about to move to Montreal. We couldn't take them along, and we couldn't expect there would be renters who'd put up with being rammed all over the place. I told Mike and Jim that they could take him. I thought they would just truck him away and turn him into food far from my sight, but Mike said, "No, the town ordinance in State College and Boalsburg prohibits slaying of cattle. We'll do it in your field."

"Fine, go ahead, as long as I don't look at it and Eva is not here, that should be all right."

"We have to skin them and let the meat cure. We'd have to hang them on one of your trees, maybe from the tree house."

"Tree house? That's my daughter's place, and to kill her pets and hang them from it is something she would really hate."

"Okay, how about in your garage?"

"Are you kidding? They are my pets as well. I am not going

to eat them, so why would I have them bleed on the cement and smell their blood below my studio. You could find some tree in the woods."

"Wouldn't a bear get them?"

"If a bear had wanted them, he would have gotten them already. Black bears are vegetarian."

"They might make an exception for fresh lamb."

"You call him a lamb?"

Mike and Jim bought a fancy butcher knife for the occasion, they read manuals on how to butcher, and they came in, looking all jaunty like real gentlemen ranchers. I sent them into the field and didn't want to pay any attention to their meat harvest but pretended in the meantime to be working on a novel; yet I could not concentrate. Five minutes later, I heard three gunshots, and I saw them running. Zidane had fallen in the driveway and the hunters were now chasing Leche in the woods. They couldn't contain Zidane in the pen; he managed to run out and they couldn't catch him, so they hunted him like a deer. But I imagined what was started had to be finished. There were three more shots in the woods and the two men kept running after Leche. I called Jeanette on the cellphone not to come back at this time, but her cellphone was off. And a minute later, she and Eva pulled in with the jeep, parked, and Jim said to Eva, don't look. Of course she looked. And when she saw Zidane, she started sobbing and trembling. She ran into the house.

"Is Leche alive?"

"Yes."

"They can't kill her!" she said.

I came out and said, "You got to stop. You can't shoot Leche."

"Okay," Mike said.

"She's just a little girl; didn't I tell you not to do it right here?"

"They escaped, what could we do?"

"Well, take him away then."

They loaded him on the back of the pickup. Jim evened out the snow where there was a lot of blood and covered the blood. They also now felt nauseated, and we all did. This was a disaster. If it had been done more discreetly, perhaps it would not have felt like such a disaster, but the fact would be the same.

Leche was spared. Instead of coming up to the upper field right by the house in the old shed below the chicken coop, she still went down into the old field to sleep. Maybe she didn't understand that Zidane was gone. And she kept sleeping there every day, and showed up only for fresh hay and grains.

Anyhow, I felt worse than I expected after Zidane was gone. Sure, now it was easy to walk across the yard and not look around for a potential attacker. We didn't need too much hay. We didn't need to keep locking up the sheep as Leche was benevolent. And soon, she seemed to thrive.

I kept seeing him, visualizing him in the field, and behind the car, his forceful and lusty nature. And I remember the last time I saw him. I had actually hoped by then that Jim and Mike had given up on coming, as they were a month late. I gave Zidane cabbage and he did not eat but followed me along the fence, and I petted him and scratched his forehead. His eyes were wet. He bowed his head and waited. As I walked up the hill he was there looking after me. It crossed my mind, what if this is the last time we look into each other's eyes? And it was. Did he understand that he was being betrayed, the quintessential human betrayal in progress?

For two months Leche stayed in the hay where she and Zidane used to sleep, waiting for him, even at night with coyotes and perhaps bears around. Later she came up, and for a few weeks, every late afternoon when I was there, she and I would run around the house in the fields. Eva ran after us, jealous that Leche came out to play with me, and after a while, Leche accepted her as part of the flock.

Eva wasn't particularly close to Zidane, but the event was a painful one for her, and it strangely mirrored my childhood. She had lost other pets—to disease, cars, and other animals—but this one was the first loss to human callousness, to the practical system of eating. And it was my betrayal. I am not sure she trusted me or other people as much after this event, just as, I suppose, I had lost some trust in my mother after my pet ram was eaten at the street corner. I had seen her chop off chicken heads on a stump with an axe, and she had taught me that eating meat followed the gory murder of animals, and perhaps that's why we ate meat only once a week. Now Eva decided to become a vegetarian, and she made exceptions, but would never eat lamb. There's incredible sadness in how most of us live, on the blood of creatures.

Life went on, almost as usual, after Zidane. Eva occasionally hugged Leche and kissed her forehead. We all ran at sunset, and Leche galloped and hopped high, like a happy lamb. And after us ran the shadow of Zidane, black head and cloudy body, bringing wetness into our eyes.

Putin's Dry Law

Now and then I plug the jug, as the expression goes. In 2006, when I went to Russia with my family, I decided that I would not drink while in Russia. We arrived in winter, and it was still dark at ten in the morning. I found a coffee house a block away from where we rented the apartment in St. Petersburg. Every day at 9 a.m., I went to the café and drank cappuccinos, and the waitresses, as soon as they saw me, would say, *Dvoynoi* cappuccino? *Da*, double, *pozhalusta*. With such good coffee I didn't miss alcohol at all, although the coffee shop offered absinthe and whisky. I was supposed to be a Fulbright research fellow, expected to give a few lectures at St. Petersburg State University, but nobody ever got in touch with me to offer me an office or to ask me to lecture, which was just fine with me. I only visited the university to have my visa extended, which a man did, without saying a word. The coffee shop would be my office, and I'd write there, but my family and I were a bit socially isolated, and so we organized a literary party. Russian poets, such as Arkady Dragomoschenko and Skidan read; my friend David Stromberg read an excerpt from his novel about an alcoholic Russian immigrant in Jerusalem; and many people I didn't know read, such as a tall and thin poet named Pavel. I got them all plenty of wine but I didn't drink any of it. Pavel did, and he vomited all over the apartment. Jeanette was scandalized—you call those people poets? They are just drunks. Don't invite them again. I'm glad that at least you're not drinking.

I was glad too. Forty days went by, and we took a train to Moscow to visit my childhood friend Bozo, the Croatian ambassador. In

Moscow both my daughter and wife got food poisoning from the food on the train. Moreover, for some reason we had a hard time finding the embassy and the street, so we wandered in deep snow against the wind. Exhausted and frozen, we were relieved to finally find my friend in a warm space, and to drink Russian tea. How about some vodka? offered Bozo. No, I don't drink at all. That's impressive, he said. The second day, Bozo said, how about some Vranac from Montenegro? It's really good. Don't tempt him, his wife said, Didn't he tell you loud and clear that he is a non-alcoholic? Yes, he did, Bozo said. I intervened, Well, the wine makes me nostalgic, I'll have just a little glass, and I'll pretend it didn't happen. I will stay on the wagon. Great idea, said Bozo, and poured me a glass; we clinked, and drank. It was good indeed. We ended up drinking, among the four adults, two bottles, and our mood was excellent. And we repeated the exercise the following evening.

Back in St. Petersburg, I didn't drink for two days, but then, we had visitors, Boris and Natasha, a violinist and his painter wife, who gave my daughter art lessons. To host them I got some red wine and cooked salmon for them. I drank too. As if to spite me, a wine shop opened across from us on Griboyedova. I bought a bunch of Spanish and Georgian wines. Now with meals we had wine: I definitely was not on the wagon, but deceived myself by declaring that I was on the moderation wagon, no more than three glasses a day. I became a regular customer at the wine shop, and sometimes, the wine was exceedingly bitter because clearly it had nearly frozen in transport, but that didn't prevent me from this form of evening relaxation.

If a politician got me off the wagon, a bigger politician intervened and threatened to help. Putin came to my aid. Namely, he outlawed all Georgian products, including the mineral water Borjomi and especially Georgian wines. For a while, all alcohol products were outlawed in Russia, and a strange disquiet wafted through the streets of St. Petersburg. People walked more quickly and aggressively than before. The newspapers gave an explanation: the government had to do a precise inventory of the stock in the country. Much of the wine was not regulated enough, so now it would be monitored better and it would be safer. By some estimates about 30,000 people had died that year from *samogon* (home-distilled moonshine) and other alcoholic products containing methyl alcohol. So, it was like another *Sukhoi Zakon*. Dry law. Gorbachev introduced it a while back and that precipitated his demise. For several days I had nothing to drink, and I was beginning to feel fresher, and thought, the hell with it, it's for the best. But on one occasion, in a 24-hour store, I noticed a few bottles of red wine, which the attendant sold me at twice the previous price. And so not even Putin could help me.

After Russia, I plugged the jug again, and I found it easy. As Mark Twain said, It's easy to quit. I have done it many times.

A Cat Named Sobaka

O n the coldest day of the year in St. Petersburg, Russia, while walking out of a tavern called Brodyachaya Sobaka (Stray Dog) with my daughter Eva and my publisher friend David, we came across a kitten shivering on a cement step along the stone wall. David picked her up.

"She could be sick," I said. "You pick her up just like that?"

"What should we do with her?" he asked.

"We'll take her. We can't let her freeze to death," I said.

"She's cute!" said Eva.

"Of course, to you all cats are cute. She's just an alley cat—tabby, scraggly."

"Look how big her stripes are, they run in circles. She's like a leopard. Let's take her home!"

"You're right. These are bold stripes."

"She must be starving," David said, or Eva said, or I said, I don't remember who. Somebody said it, and we all meant it, and so we took her to the first place along the way where you could buy cheap food, a coffee place near Shostakovich Hall, where Eva and I had heard Anne-Sophie Mutter perform Mozart sonatas delicately. The kitten climbed David; he had a worsted wool sweater, and she must have liked the warmth. David grinned happily.

"Is it a boy or a girl?" Eva asked.

"A girl, because she likes guys. She likes David."

"Not all girls like guys," she said, "I don't." Eva was reaching over and petting the kitten who didn't seem to understand petting. She shivered and purred and blinked. Her eyes were teary. She sneezed.

"She doesn't seem all that healthy," I reasserted my impression.

The otherwise bored and pained waitresses, who looked like retired models, tilting their hips, with half-moons sagging below their eyes, came over, and I thought they would want us to throw the kitten out. That's what had happened to me and a beige cat at Starbucks in State College—the manager came over and asked me to leave with the cat. People could be allergic, he said, it's against the rules. Well, I happen to be allergic to silly rules, I said. I get all itchy when I hear an unnecessary rule. Yes, those were the rules back in our boastfully free country, but here in Russia, the land of the non-free, the cat was welcome. Nobody sneezed. Or that is, they sneezed all the time, so there was no point in isolating causes. *Ochen krasivaya*, said one dirty-blond waitress. *Milaya*. The other waitress stretched over the table and petted the kitten, brushing me with her hip in passing.

"What's her name?" she asked.

"We don't know yet," I said. "You have a suggestion?"

"I'll think about it," she said. "Now I have to go back to the customers."

Before naming her, we needed to feed her. We got her a bit of milk and a meat pierogi. She sniffed at the milk and sneezed. She chewed a little meat, and could barely swallow, and then trembled as though it was too much for her body.

"Maybe she's too weak to eat," I said.

Maybe she had a bad relationship with her mom, and so she hates milk. If she were in New York, we could put her in psychotherapy until she forgave her mother. She still shivered and sneezed. Mist blasted from her nostrils.

"She would have died for sure if we hadn't picked her up," David said. "Should we name her Prokofiev?"

"Just Coffee Bean?" Eva said.

"Maybe Masha?" I said. "What do Russians name their cats?"

"Murmansk, because to them *mur* is purr. Mura," David suggested.

"No, that won't do. How about Sobaka," I said.

"That's awkward. She's not a dog. That might doom her to the life of a dog."

"Yes, but we found her at the Stray Dog tavern, so why not Sobaka? Sobaka seems to like you. Do you want to take her home?"

"But Daddy, I want a kitten."

"Mom will be mad at us if we bring her home."

"Yes, I'd like her," David said. He took off his black-framed glasses and wiped them with his sleeve, his eyes a bit teary. "I always had cats as a kid. You sure you don't want her?"

"You saw her first and you have a kid. Shakhar would like her."

"Let me call my girlfriend," he said. After the call, he said, "We need to think about it. For now, why don't you keep her and if I can take her later, I will."

"That's great, Daddy, we'll take care of her."

We brought her home, and Jeanette said, "She looks sickly. Look at her eyes. She's so thin, maybe has distemper."

"Well, what do you suggest we do?"

"I don't think Eva should be touching her. Put her in some kind of animal shelter. Russians must have one."

"Yes, it's called the gas chamber. No, we have to take care of her."

Eva, of course, couldn't keep her hands off the kitten. Sobaka ran, jumped, chased candy wrappers on the floor and purred as soon as you looked at her. She would come to my ear and stick her nose in. The nose was wet and it tickled me. I laughed.

I bought a tetracycline cream for the eyes and rubbed the cream in a few times a day but she still sneezed all the time and couldn't keep her food down—she either vomited or had diarrhea. The

137

piano teacher who visited us gave us an address for a vet. But the kitten's health gradually improved. Her eyes didn't water as much and she sneezed less and less.

Eva had a friend, Sarah, who was wild about Sobaka. Sarah was tall for her age and slim. She came over for play dates. Eva and she raised hell together. For Eva's birthday, they opened the window of our rented apartment, and shouted, *Privet, Sankt Petersburg. Davay tvoj cigaret!* They shrieked and giggled and pretended to be smoking. Our apartment looked right out onto the legendary Nevsky Prospekt where revolutions had taken place. Now, a new revolution was in evidence—lots of people in mink coats, Hummers, the new oil money spilling all over, ostentatiously bypassing the majority of still shabbily dressed people.

Eva's Russian pronunciation was perfect even if her vocabulary wasn't.

Sobaka grew healthy and shiny although she was a little too slim. I took her to the vet to get shots, but the vet said that for a rabies vaccine, the kitten had to be six months old. She gave me a prescription for worms, and insisted that I get a German one, rather than the Russian pill. Bayer makes the best deworming medicine. In general, I found out that the Russians seem to admire everything made in Germany. While waiting for the exam, I saw that Sobaka was most likely a breed of sorts, a Bengali cat. She looked like an alley cat, but she had those stripes that whorled around, bold against a somewhat orange backdrop.

I took Sobaka for trips across the town, when Eva went to see Sarah. In the *marshutkas* (minibuses or vans), she'd stay quiet for ten minutes and then she'd howl.

She peeked out of my bag and generally caught the attention of passengers, who seemed to like cats. There were cats everywhere in Russia, many of whom were strays. There were stray dogs too, some of them quite beautiful. In Moscow, Eva struck up a friendship with a dog amidst the rush-hour traffic, after we got kicked out of a hotel because the university offices hadn't yet returned my visa registration slip, and therefore I couldn't register to stay in any hotel. Luckily my phone had just enough time for me to call a friend of mine, the Croatian ambassador, who would put us up for two days. The beige dog made eye contact with Eva and followed us. He looked very reasonable. How could he navigate the subway system? For us it was hard. I remember a friend of mine, Joyce, had a dog in Berlin, whom she could leave at a subway stop and he'd go home. He could either read German or smell the right subway stop. Maybe each subway stop had its own smell. Eva cried when we told her she had to break up the new friendship. Anyway, Russians like cats even more than dogs—that was my vague impression. I admired the city cats. Each enclosed yard, constituting about a quarter of the city block, with apartment buildings encircling it, contained a whole cat culture: the strays, who lived in a variety of holes, in the garbage dump; the indoor-outdoor cats; and the purely indoor cats, who stared out like privileged Americans in a gated community, scared to get out into the rough world.

Sobaka underwent the quick conversion from an outdoor stray to the indoor gated type of cat. Actually, I suspected that she had been an indoor type, but because of her eye infection, she was thrown out and abandoned near the type of café frequented by foreigners who might pick her up. The apartment had a balcony which we didn't use in the winter but when the spring came, we opened it up, and occasionally let Sobaka out. The balcony was on the second floor, but the yard cats managed to climb up and hiss at Sobaka, who was eager to play with other cats and was quite put off by this expression of animosity. St. Petersburg is traditionally a revolutionary city, and classes are full of hatred for one another here, and cats, who in many ways reflect human societies, apparently are also highly class-conscious and inimical to those of other classes. A calico came over and hissed every morning.

Some strays didn't do well. On the way to Eva's school, we saw a dead cat thrown into the river, or rather onto the ice covering the river. The river was completely frozen over, and it had a layer of snow on top of the ice. Near the bridge there were cigarette butts and beer cans frozen in ice, sticking out, and past them this dead black and white cat. Maybe she froze to death. Maybe she was beaten to death. Maybe a dog killed her. Maybe she was sick. Maybe she died of old age. Does anybody die of old age?

Once in the street I happened to lift my gaze, perhaps because I saw some motion, and there was a cat flying, falling. I stretched out my arms and caught her. A young woman shouted from the window, It's my cat. O.K., come and get her, I said, and she did. The woman grabbed the cat, said *spasiba*, and ran back into the courtyard.

Our landlady was friendly to the idea of a cat. She asked where the cat pooped, and I showed her a litter box in the bathroom. Margarita was impressed. She sniffed and said, *Zapaha nyet.* It doesn't stink.

For some reason Sobaka had a long-lasting diarrhea. My impression of Russia was that it was a common affliction among people and animals alike, with giardia and all sorts of parasites. And sometimes Sobaka missed the spot, or the bathroom would be mistakenly closed, and she liked one corner particularly, over the vents.

She often slept at my feet, and like most cats, she perceived human feet to be separate individuals; toes were the targets.

Eva wanted me to bring Sobaka to the States. Now, almost anything that can be complicated is complicated in Russia. I had to get a passport for the cat, clearly identifying her, listing her shots, and so on. I went to the veterinarian, and there waited among a variety of people and their pets. It was incredibly hot in the waiting room, and the Russians didn't seem to mind that but I had to walk out to breathe and get some cold water. The sight outside, when I crossed the bridge on the Griboyedova, was fantastic—straight ahead the golden dome of St. Paul's cathedral, gleaming. The canal zigzagged and there were three bridges crossing the canal at various angles. It's easy to get lost here, unless you have a clear view of the orienting spires. Now that it was spring, there were people walking everywhere. I went back to the hot and steamy vet's office.

The vet said, "What's your cat's name?"

"Sobaka," I said.

"That won't do. You can't name a cat Dog."

"But I have."

"She must have a less confusing name, officially."

"All right, Olga."

"That's a human name."

"Nobody will mistake her for a human."

"That's true. Fine."

She wrote Olga Novakovich in Cyrillic. She also gave the cat a variety of shots. She wrote a few certificates, and stamped them. Russians believe in stamps and seals. Everything must be documented.

I also had to take a cello out of the country. It was imprisoned because we didn't have the proper papers for it. Friends of ours kept it, and now I had to go to the culture ministry and have the cello assessed. I paid ten per cent of the declared value for the exit visa for the cello. The photographer took front, back and sideways shots, and the assessor described the cracks. Meanwhile, a Dutch violinist was crying because the border guards wouldn't let her take out the violin, although it was hers, and her flight was leaving in the afternoon. I don't know whether she got the papers to leave the country, but I suspect that with a ten-per cent payment, she was allowed to take it out, and hopefully it wasn't worth too much.

And precisely because of the weeping and crying possibilities, one could get a pet exit visa validated only one day before departure at the airport. It wouldn't do to have a pet rejected for a trip and the owner getting on the plane and abandoning the pet. Still, it seemed strange that there was no office downtown to verify the papers. I had to take Sobaka to the airport twice this way. At least I knew how to take *marshutkas* so I wouldn't have to pay too much in cab fares to the airport. It used to be cheap to go to the airport by cab, but now it could cost thirty dollars each way.

After getting all these papers it was almost a letdown that I got onto the Pulkovo airplane without anybody asking about the cat or noticing that there was a cat at the ticket counter; and at security, I asked for the cat not to go through the X-rays, and the guards took her out, petted her, put her back in the box. On the airplane my neighbours didn't pay any attention to Sobaka. They were busy planning a biking trip around Normandy. I talked to them a little. One woman was a hotel manager, the Karamazov Hotel. Russians now travelled with a vengeance, and there was a sort of middle class that suddenly made real money, which made it possible to travel.

In Paris I barely made the connecting flight. Again, nobody paid any attention to my having a cat, and I didn't have to pay a fee. By the rules, I probably should have paid the fee. Anyhow, I had the most certified cat in the Western Hemisphere now. The cat charmed the stewardesses. I took her to the toilet to pee. I had brought some sand and her box, and she did fine, but on the descent, there was a sudden stinging stink. Sobaka was terrified of the descent. She meowed. Her previous friend, the stewardess, laughed when she smelled it and waved her hand in front of her nose like a fan.

I landed in Chicago, and proudly I flashed papers: my cat was certified. I declared I had a pet and the officer said, You need to get the papers examined, and he directed me to a vet room, but then called me back. It's just a cat? And you have the papers and shots? O.K., just go through, no problem.

I drove her to Pennsylvania, her new home. *Nastayescha Amerikanka*, future American, that's what I called her for a while. I had to leave right away to teach a brief course in Minnesota, and I left Sobaka locked in the basement. My wife and daughter would come in a couple of days. I couldn't let Sobaka roam freely because a cat needs about three days to establish a sense of home well enough to be able to return to it by whatever magnetic or memory means. So for a while I listened to reports about how Sobaka was doing. I expected she would love the outdoors after a brief adjustment but she was very cautious at first. Although she was initially most likely an outdoor cat, the outdoors scared her. Well, she was a cosmopolitan cat, and these were the boonies with all sorts of smells and creatures. When she did go outside, the other cats didn't welcome her. I thought that with her wild genes of a Bengali cat, she would have some real leopard ancestors, which I thought would give her the edge. But other cats, especially Jacqueline (named after du Pré, the cellist), chased her and treed her. Sobaka climbed our tallest tree, above the roof of our house, and she didn't know how to get back to the ground. There was thunder and lightning, which must have terrified her, but still, she didn't dare go down the tree. She stayed there for four days, and Jeanette thought of calling the fire-fighters to get her out of the tree, but she wasn't sure they could do it, as the tree was on a slippery slope after the rains. After five days, she came down, a bit thinner than before. Now the other cats growled at her but didn't chase her off. Sobaka was about eight months old but seemed younger—somehow she had stopped growing rapidly. Maybe she was older when we found her than we thought.

She was a shy cat, less charismatic than she'd been in Russia. She roamed in the woods, and tried to catch birds and squirrels.

I was sure that eventually her leopard nature would kick in—first she needed to grow. I looked forward to her becoming a mother, wondering what her kittens would look like when combined with our orange tomcat's. They would be wonderful. When the first round of mating took place, she was curious. Augustine was mating with Jacqueline. Later she emitted her meows, as if to say, How about me? Don't you like brunettes as well?

With my daughter Eva and me, she played kitty-pong. She sat in the middle of the table and tried to catch the balls. She'd jump to catch the balls like a goalkeeper. Frequently she managed to kick them that way, and then she'd jump off the table and chase them. Sometimes she lay along the net and travelled by sliding alongside it, helping herself along with her claws in the net. We didn't mind the net getting wrecked because it was so cute.

Once she disappeared and Eva and I grieved. Why didn't I let her in? I had heard her late at night and it was cold outside. Maybe she took a trip. I don't know where she went but she came back.

"I am so relieved," Eva said. We combed Sobaka, and she purred. "Look how healthy she is—her eyes are so clear, her fur is shiny."

"How many lives has she spent?" Eva wondered. "Let's see, one in Russia, when she was freezing to death; another, when she was recovering from her distemper; the third, when she came down the tree after being up there for five days; and this was the fourth. She has five more lives."

"That's pretty good, better than us."

Eva was wild about animals. Her complaint once when she found a snake in Nebraska wasn't that the snake bit her but that it left her and slithered away into the bushes. The bite had startled her so she dropped the snake. If she had her way, we'd turn our house into a zoo. Sobaka was our Russian link, and we were proud that we saved her from tyranny and brought her into democracy, where if the people's will was to be done, she'd be immediately spayed. No doubt, that wouldn't be the will of the cat. We thought we would spay her, but first it would be good to get some of her exotic kittens. They would be story kittens, because they would have her background and the chilly Russian roots.

The more time she spent outdoors, the more she liked it, and she ran around, especially after birds. We realized that kitty-pong was good training, unfortunately, for bird hunting. Still, she caught no birds. The weather was turning cold. We used to have a cat in Ohio, also a tabby, who was a clever hunter. She hid in a tiger-lily bush, where the bright colours attracted hummingbirds, and to our despair, she caught two hummingbirds. Would Sobaka turn out to be like that? There were woodpeckers, cardinals, indigo buntings. Woodpeckers could take care of themselves.

The cold brought along the hunting season. We were afraid that our orange tomcat, who roamed far and wide in search of his genetic destiny—the goal was perhaps to have ten percent of the cats in the fifty-mile radius carry his genetic imprint. Supposedly, in Mongolia, eight per cent of the people are Genghis Khan's descendants. On Bald Eagle Mountain Ridge, if things keep going the way they do, in a few years there will be hundreds of Augustine's descendants. The hunters have always left Augustine alone. He comes home scratched, with torn ears from his erotic endeavours.

So when Sobaka disappeared for two days again, there was no worry about the hunters. Jeanette says that she heard meowing late one night but was too sleepy to go downstairs to see which cat it was, and as it was a warm night, that should not have been a problem. In the morning, however, she found Sobaka in the woodpile, and around her and near the door, there was blood. Sobaka appeared to have a bullet hole in her side. Probably a hunter shot her.

When I got home, I found a loose tree stump, and pulled it out, which, in the rocky terrain, was the best way to have a relatively deep hole. I deepened it and widened it and we placed the poor creature into it. There was a white film over her eyes, which stayed open.

"Should we close the eyes?" asked Eva.

"What do you think? It makes no difference."

"Do you want to examine her wound?"

"No. I believe Mom. It's a bullet hole. I am a little queasy from the sadness."

"Can I touch her and kiss her?"

"No, she's been dead too long. It's not a good idea."

Eva wept.

"Do you want to say a prayer for her?" I asked.

"I don't know any. You do."

"Yes, but I think it's too late for that."

"I'll smoke a cigarette for her," she said.

"Where will you find one?"

"Mom has some in your room."

She brought out the cigarette, and I let her smoke it, and the smoke stung her eyes, and she wept from the grief and the stinging, and coughed and sniffled.

We put Sobaka in the soil, where she did not belong. I put stones, mud, and broken tree roots over her body in a shoebox. We also put a yellow ping-pong ball in there, so she would have something to play with in the afterlife.

Crossbar

I n a semi-final UEFA Cup match in Maksimir, Dinamo Zagreb trailed Crvena Zvezda Belgrade 1 to 2. Ten minutes before the end of regulation time, Zvezda's halfback Milic deflected the ball with his hand. The Dutch referee should have blown a whistle for a penalty, but he didn't. Was it possible that he didn't see the hand-play, and that the assistant referees hadn't either, while the whole stadium had? The fans were shrieking and throwing firecrackers and for a few minutes the match was suspended, and after a deliberation, the referees decided to let the game resume.

Big guys around me kept jumping so that the cement stands shook. I have no idea how these guys grew up to be like bears—most of them in the range of 6' 2" to 6' 6" and weighing between 250 and 350 pounds. It looked unseemly that such huge guys would be passionate about what short and stringy fellows did in the grass with a few balls. I was one of those guys, jumping and shrieking. Ordinarily I was a civilized writer, with a taste for macchiato and single malts, and at the beginning of the match I still was a civilized human. But by the end, I had taken off my shirt and was hollering for blood.

The game became frenetic. See, I am cultured enough to use words like that (and I am even writing this whole thing in English, not all that patriotic of me) when I am away from the stadium. But in it, I am a Roman barbarian, wanting to see gladiators kick balls like chopped heads. Dinamo exerted fantastic pressure, shooting at the goal almost twice a minute, and then there was a great chance as Hodzic passed all the players, advancing to the goal. He was felled by Branislav Ivanovic, who slid into his shins. Ivanovic is a fine player, Chelsea captain until recently, and I am sure he intended to get the ball rather than the player, but at that speed it's impossible to always be accurate. Anyhow, it was a clear penalty, and strangely enough, the stingy Dutch referee did whistle and point to the penalty spot. Hodzic, the new phenomenal player for Dinamo, got the honour of shooting.

I knew that Hodzic probably hated the Serbian players. Hodzic was born in 1992 in a Croatian village near Bugojno in Bosnia, and both of his parents were executed in front of him. He was raised by his grandmother, as a refugee in Austria, and for him, eliminating Zvezda must have been a dream.

At the whistle, Hodzic ran, took a full swing at the ball, and the ball flew straight and hit the inside of the crossbar in the right corner. The metal resounded. The ball bounced onto the line and back up to the crossbar. The Zvezda goalie, instead of catching the ball now, kicked it out and it landed on Hodzic's chest. Hodzic had another chance: he shot and yet again hit the crossbar, and the ball flew far out, where Ivanovic cleared it, sending it away into the Dinamo stands. Now you had to admire Hodzic's shots, even though they didn't go in. I think that there should be a different scoring system, whereby each hit on the crossbar should count as half a point. Three crossbar hits would have amounted to 1.5 goals and Dinamo would have made it. Anyway, the crowd was in a wounded state. In the stinging smokescreen, anything could happen, and it did. Many of us jumped over the fence, and right in front of me, I saw a man with a machete. Another one grabbed the referee, the Dutchman by the august name of Rembrandt, pushed him to the ground, onto his knees, and the first one brought the machete down, beheading him. Somehow it looked normal, at first . . . easy. The head fell and rolled and ended up sideways in the grass, stopped by the hooked nose.

I followed another group of hooligans, who got hold of the Dinamo players and beat them systematically. Somebody knocked

Hodzic down, and several people kicked him, shouting insults: scumbag, good-for-nothing, they bribed you, didn't they? fucking whore. . . . One of them said, I have a better idea, let's take him to the zoo.

I think I'd had a whole bottle of Hennessy during the game, and instead of sobering up upon seeing the beheading, I went along with the hooligans. Hell, I was one of them. I must admit, I even gave Hodzic a kick, somewhere in the kidney area, and I was one of the guys carrying him to the zoo. There were five of us, like pall-bearers. The zoo had modernized recently. It used to have barred cages, but now, with Croatia being a member of the E.U., the zoo had become more humane, and tigers got a bigger cage: an acre of land, with trees to sharpen their claws, with a little pond to drink water from and bathe in—and these were new Siberian tigers, Putin's present to Croatia.

Anyway, we tried to toss Hodzic over the fence into the cage, but the fence was too tall, and Hodzic fell out of our hands onto the pavement. He shrieked. Oh, shut up, you should have kicked that ball a little lower. Why go that high with it?

Let's take him to the grizzlies, someone proposed. And we went on and carried Hodzic to the grizzly cage. These august creatures were a political present too, from Obama. There was a long tradition of presents from other countries in the form of animals. Indira Gandhi had given elephants, Mao Tse Tung panda bears, and these grizzlies as well, named Bill and Hillary. Anyway, these guys were massive, the male probably 800 pounds and the female 450, even bigger than Siberian tigers.

We had to climb the fence to throw him down. He landed on the rocks, a little island. Bill and Hillary jumped to the island and sniffed Hodzic. We shouted, tear him, eat him, but the bears merely sniffed him all over for a while, and then licked his face. They did not bite him. Hodzic didn't move, sprawled and loose like a rag doll. Bill roared at us, jumped at the fence, growled at us, and jumped again. He managed to climb the fence, and soon he jumped over it, and knocked down one guy and snapped his neck. I ran. He bit my right calf and tore it right out. I pissed in terror and ran out of the zoo and into the streets, and a cab driver, who was right there near the zoo entrance, gave me a ride to the Rebro hospital. I bled richly and groaned until they cut off the circulation to my leg, and gave me shots to stop the bleeding, and then morphine too. At first it had hurt less than I imagined it should—the shock is a natural painkiller—and that's how I had managed to run for my life. I passed out at the hospital from morphine and the loss of blood. When I woke up, I was in horrifying pain; my nerves were severed too, and I got more morphine. I stayed in the hospital for days. The surgeons patched me up, and now without these muscles, it was clear I would limp for the rest of my life. At least I had the rest of my life. I wondered how Hodzic was doing and I looked it up online.

Hodzic had a broken spine, a concussion, broken ribs, and a ruptured kidney. He was in critical condition at the Rebro hospital. Thank god we didn't kill him. I swore I would never watch another soccer game if I could help it, and I would never root again for any team. Croatia, both individual teams and the national team, was banned from international competition for four years anyway. If I hadn't been there, the same thing would have happened—there were enough hooligans. Maybe I shouldn't feel terribly guilty, but of course I should.

When I recovered enough, I volunteered to take Hodzic around in a wheelchair, and we became fast friends. I took him to Gradska Kavana every morning for macchiato. Because of spinal cord damage, he'd never be able to walk again unless medicine improves.

And what did we talk about? Anything but soccer. For a whole year I couldn't bring myself to tell him that I was one of the thugs.

But one day, when we were relaxing and in a particularly fabulous mood, he suggested we go to the zoo. "I want to say hi to Bill and Hillary. You know, she saved my life by licking me and nursing me. I think I was clinically dead; I saw my dad and mom in heaven, and we ate baklava together. I think there's life after death."

We took a cab. On the right side was the Dinamo stadium. He turned away from it. "I don't want to see that again."

I helped him get out of the cab with his electric wheelchair, and we went past the Siberian tigers, to the bears. I had no reason to be glad to see them, but Hodzic shouted, "Hello, my friends!" Both bears stood on their hind legs and made strange noises, something between a growl and a roar, but a couple of octaves higher, the way they would talk to a cub.

"Beautiful, aren't they?" he said. "See, they remember me. Next time I am going to bring them some trout."

"You aren't supposed to feed them."

"I can do what I want. You'll help me get here?"

"Of course."

"What would I do without you?"

"You know, Bill ate my right calf. I am not that eager to feed him. I already did."

"I know. I've read the articles."

"You knew it all along. How? That's crazy. Why would you talk to me then?"

"I saw the pictures, security-camera pictures, and I could tell that one of the silhouettes was you. And then there were articles about the bear, how he killed two hooligans and tore up your leg."

"And you don't blame me?"

"Of course I blame you, you ass, but I understand. You were a fucking hooligan, You weren't the ringleader anyway."

"Generous interpretation."

"Not generous. Let me show you something." He leaned over,

opened his jacket—and I could see he carried an Uzi. "Guess what that is for?"

"Security?"

"No. I am waiting for the other two. You are O.K., you suffered, and I got to know you. Bill avenged me, and you weren't the ringleader, but when I see those motherfuckers, off they go."

"Wow!"

"It's vow, not wow. So when can you come back to feed Bill and Hill with me?"

"I'm not sure. Seeing that gun makes me lose the appetite for it."

And as I stared at him, looking kind of like Stephen Hawking in his wheelchair, with thick glasses, and a proper black jacket, with a red tie, I imagined I was seeing him for the last time. But am I stuck with him now? If I quit seeing him, will he put me on the list of people to shoot? With thoughts like these, we couldn't be friends anymore.

"Adios, my friend!" I said, and turned my back to him, my hard-sole leather shoes crunching the sharp gravel, with every little stone imprinting itself into the skin of my feet as I angled to walk away. An uneasy feeling chilled my back, as though a bullet would go through me at any second.

Tumbling: Croatia

That's where my father and I differ, although people tell me we look alike. Namely, he was an herbalist, and drank close to a hundred different varieties of tea, which still didn't spare him from a massive heart attack. I wonder whether drinking a hundred varieties of wine would have worked better. Anyhow, cardiology has advanced a lot since those days, and I've had the honour of travelling to Croatia and Bosnia with a photographer, Jon Hughes, from Cincinnati, who warned me, "I will come, but I know the region is famous for unrestrained drinking and I want none of that. I've had heart failure, and I carefully balance my chemistry with lipitor and amlodipine, cholesterol and blood pressure meds. I will not drink in your fucking country."

"Jon, why would I care? Drink tea if you like, there's lots of it. I don't plan to drink anything either, you know, but I can't guarantee it won't happen."

I'd already had a couple of glasses of red wine on our flight to relieve my anxiety.

"I couldn't do that," Jon said. He took melatonin and slept through the entire flight.

We rented a car in Frankfurt, and he drove at first as I hadn't slept, and was legally intoxicated. One of our first stops was Vodnjan, to visit my friend Boris.

Boris said, "You look like the road sucked the life out of you. I'll get you some wine from our neighbour."

He went to the shop next door and brought four litres of red wine, and declared that the whole deal was only four bucks.

"Why so much wine?" asked Jon. "I ain't gonna drink none of it."

"Oh, shush," I said. "You never know. I will." I tasted it. It was simple, airy, like some kind of Bourgogne or Beaujolais, and it tasted good. One gulp was lonely and it begged for another, and I downed an entire refreshing glass, and said to Jon, "All right, my friend, just have a sip. I swear, the wine is thin, won't affect your heart at all."

"You know, you sluts, you've aroused my curiosity," he said, and he tasted the wine from a regular waterglass. "Oh well, I've blown my wine cherry. I haven't had a sip in a year and here I go. My doctor would not be happy."

"Of course he'd be happy," I said. "Either you earn another bypass surgery or you get cured. Either he makes a ton of money off you, or he can boast that he's a good doctor. And what do you think he would do? WWJD? Is that it, What would Jesus do? He would drink some and talk to his Dad. Well, I envy him there, I can't talk to mine, but that's beside the point? Refill?"

"Oh yeah," said Jon, and smiled and his eyes vanished and his moustache spread its wings like a bird in Texas. I have no idea why I wrote Texas, but who cares.

I went back to the store before it closed, and the young man put more wine into 1.5-litre Coca-Cola bottles. Boris's neighbour, sitting on his steps that hot night in a wife-beater shirt, looked at me and said, "Why red wine? White is better."

"That's a matter of taste," I said.

"Is there something wrong with your blood? My wife is anaemic, although she now and then flares up and throws things at me, and she doesn't look anaemic to me, but the doctor says she is, and prescribes red wine. If something's wrong with your blood, you drink red wine. But just to relax and cool off, of course you drink white wine."

"So what's your favourite?" I asked.

"Don't have one. I hate all alcohol and haven't had a sip of all that shit in my entire life. I've seen what it does to people."

"Okay, so why talk to me about it?" I wanted to say something unprintable, but he looked so good and meek and soulful, sitting on the second stone stair, in his red shorts and white wife-beater, hairy, squat, that I only said, "Good night."

Jon must have had the equivalent of three traditional bottles of red wine. He said, "I'm sorry and I'm not. I feel good." In the morning, he said, "I feel good. Can we drink more of that?"

We drove to Sarajevo. I stressed Jon out by driving on *Jadranska magistrala*, before the new highways were built, very competitively, and he said, "You pass another car like that on a curve, and I am out of here."

"Oh no, you aren't. We have that tranquilizing wine," I said.

We arrived in Sarajevo and our idea of a present was ten litres of the domestic wine from Istria. My nephew, a Baptist minister, said, "You know, usually I would say no, as we are pretty strict with alcohol here, but I am so nostalgic for Croatia that I accept your gift with gratitude."

Jon and I drank our present to him and his church, at least half of it, a little sheepishly, but Jon said, "Man, I miss this wine."

"No you don't. You are drinking it!"

The next day, Jon and I drove from Sarajevo to Orasje to cross into Croatia, and we were going to pass through Republika Srpska. I didn't know that there was no checkpoint between the two parts of Bosnia. I had a book listing 3,000 slain Croatian civilians by Serbian forces in Croatia. I thought if the Serbian police searched us, they might not appreciate such a book, and I tossed it into the bushes at the curve. Republika Srpska was quiet; several Orthodox churches were being built. An old man walked two pigs on the side of the road, letting them graze in the grassy ditches.

"I feel sorry for the pigs," I said. "Probably some holiday is coming up and he's gonna roast them."

In Orasje we waited for a ferry to cross the river Sava, amidst diesel clouds of tractor-trailers. Jon said, "The beauty is that diesel is not harmful."

"I don't believe that. I am getting a headache."

"That's just wine withdrawal. By the way," Jon said. "I am done with wine. It was good while it lasted, and I would drink more of that fine young red wine, but anyhow, I am done."

"I am done too," I said. "The hell with drinking."

On the highway of Brotherhood and Unity in Croatia, I drove steadily at 130 km an hour, passing a column of trucks, which went about 80. It was already nighttime, the sky starry and indigo. A car behind me flashed at me to move over, but I wasn't going to move over and then brake in a small space between two trucks, so I kept going, accelerating to 140. That was not good enough for the BMW, which tailgated us and flashed it lights.

"That's really uncomfortable," Jon said. "He's maybe only a metre behind us."

I pulled to the right lane when I passed the first truck, and I slowed down to 130. The BMW slowed to 130 and drove in parallel. I slowed down to 100, so did the driver. I looked over, and saw a gun, probably an Uzi, pointing at me. The driver was leaning his arm on the chest of a reclining blonde woman. I accelerated, and so did he. I was back at 140, and so was he. There was no traffic on the road any more in either direction.

Jon said, "What the fuck? We're both in the line of fire. He could kill us just like that?"

"Yeah, who would know? After we're shot he could drive away, and nobody would know who did it."

"Driving can't be that serious," Jon said.

I looked over again, and I couldn't make out the features of the man very well, other than a bit of the whites of the eyes. But the gun barrel and its black hole were all too clearly visible. There were lampposts on the side of the road shedding some light, every 100 metres or so.

"He's enjoying this," Jon said. "I am not! You think he'll shoot?"

"I have no idea. The world is full of idiots. This is Texas-style road rage."

And we drove like that for a while, accelerating and decelerating, and then he suddenly accelerated to probably more than 220 km an hour and disappeared.

"God, that nearly gave me a heart attack," Jon said. "I hope the fucker crashes at the next curve."

I stayed calm through the whole thing because it was all too absurd, and I was not in control. But now I was a bit jittery, and I drove slowly the rest of the way. We came to my mother's place in Daruvar late at night. The bell didn't work, so I threw little stones and my mother opened the window and let us in. After the usual hugs, she offered us walnut strudels and tea.

Jon asked, "Can you ask her whether she has any wine? I am still shaking from that BMW."

"You have any wine, Ma?"

"Yes, a local *daruvarski* Riesling. But you know, you shouldn't be drinking."

"Will white wine do?" I asked Jon.

"Yes!"

I had a glass, and Jon had the rest of the bottle. It was quite refreshing, pretty dry and yet fruity with hints of apple and persimmon. Jon gulped and then smiled so that his eyes vanished for a while in the folds of his cheeks, and his moustache spread like the wings of a bird over Texas.

Prepaid Reservation

Not having seen my old friend Mile for 25 years, I eagerly got together with him near the fountain square in Belgrade. He hadn't changed much, other than having gained more territory—bigger bulk and presence. He'd lost most of his hair on top, and his temple hair and sideburns, white and silvery, gave him an aura of wisdom. A white beard capped his chin, like an inverse mountain peak. He had grown up without siblings near my hometown in Croatia, and perhaps because of that, he'd been extraordinarily quiet in conversations, especially philosophical ones, during which he smiled and looked at the whitewashed ceiling and a naked orange light bulb hanging on a thick curved wire. Later on he studied Phys. Ed., on account of his strength, and worked as a bouncer in a Zagreb disco before taking up a job in Mihokovicevo at a high school, from where he disappeared in 1990, before the Serbian "revolution" in Croatia.

According to rumours, he may have joined the Serbian paramilitary. Anyhow, he settled somewhere around Belgrade. The war over, I thought friendship should be stronger than ethnic divides and judgement, so I ignored the issue of how he'd spent the early nineties. I came to Belgrade to see him, along with another old friend, a publisher, and my first and unrequited love from when I was fourteen, a girl who had a wonderful gap between her front teeth. No matter what, I was eager to see Mile and I trusted he was a good man, and not a war criminal. He had actually got in touch with me, on Facebook, where his pictures of hiking in the Greek and Italian and Austrian—but certainly not Croatian—mountains popped up. I was a bit anxious before meeting him, but as soon as I saw him, we resumed communicating as though we had seen each other only a few days ago, starting with delighted smiles (his teeth were still good) and firm handshakes.

"Ah, there you are," he said. "You are the same as before, same presence, aura."

"Yes, same aura perhaps. But you haven't changed, except for the better. You look calmer and more solid. You speak Serbian *ekavica*, though."

"Well, I live in Serbia, why wouldn't I?"

"Makes sense. But our friend Dule—remember him? a history teacher—speaks Croatian, still. He says he's too old to change anything, and he has no ideology."

"I had a lot of ideology, let me tell you, when we were chased out of Croatia."

"Of course. Were you really chased out? And by whom?"

"Let's not get into that, not right away. After what happened to us Serbs in World War Two in Croatia—*Ustashas* killed my grandfather and two uncles—we were quick to respond to any threat. Both the Croatian locals and the Serbian army officers told us to clear out."

"You didn't have to. Many Serbs remained and they are fine."

"That was unpredictable. Anyway, I like it here, and I now belong. And I spent more than a year in the army here in the seventies, and I fell in love with Serbian dialects."

"I know. I visited you in the Zemun barracks."

"Did you?"

For a second I wasn't sure. Maybe I had visited only Mladen, another Serbian friend of mine, who had spent a couple of years in a lunatic asylum before killing himself. Oh yes, I definitely did visit Mile too. It was a quiet visit, and we sat on a log in the middle of the barracks. Mile didn't say much, but sat sulking, and advised me to avoid joining the army at all costs.

Now we sat in front of a café along Kneza Mihajlova (Prince Mihailo Street). For a second, we both had nothing to say as two tall ladies strutted by.

"And you see, we always have *lepe devojke*."

"Yes, I know. Once a friend of mine from New York visited me, and we walked around Belgrade, and I said, The guys in Yugoslavia seem to think they are very manly and handsome. I couldn't really judge, are they? I am not sure, she said. The women look so great, I've had no time to look at the men."

"She's right," Mile said. "Why do you think there are so many people sitting in cafés?"

After we covered many subjects in our conversation (mountain climbing, soccer violence, current elections), he said, "You are coming to sleep at my place, aren't you?"

"No, I have a reservation at a downtown hotel. Pretty fancy. In Dedinje."

"Cancel that. It's a boring bourgeois neighbourhood. Milosevic's clan lives up there. Your Croatian buddy, Byeli, is buried there."

"But it's elegant, and I am curious, and I have already paid."

"Come on, you should have consulted me first. Of course I expected you to stay with me. What kind of host do you think I am?"

"Maybe we could go to your house for a bit and you can bring me back to Belgrade."

"Once you visit me, you'll change your mind, you'll see. I've built a nice place in Pancevo, with a little vineyard and a bread oven."

"Well, I need to be in Belgrade at ten in the morning. I am meeting . . ."

"We can easily make it back by ten."

"I don't want you to cook for me, though. Let's find a good fish restaurant. I heard there's one on the Danube."

"There's a splendid one just on the other side, before Pancevo, on the way to my place. That's a great idea."

We walked down the streets, past the old *Politika* newspaper offices, and he said, "Do you know it used to be only one page? You know, like *Abendblatt, blatt* meaning a page. So the Second World War was announced just on one page."

"Oh, you know what I'd like to do? Let's visit the Cathedral of Sveti Savo. I enjoy places of worship in big cities."

"We don't have enough time for it. You won't believe me, but I haven't been there yet."

"Fine, we'll go and stay silent there for a while. Will do us good."

"Here's my car. Well, not mine, but let's say it is for a few days."

It was a silver Volkswagen Golf hatchback. Mile pulled out slowly. "I haven't driven in a year. My cousin lent me this one in Novi Sad."

"Why haven't you driven in a while?"

"I had an accident and destroyed a Golf, made in Sarajevo, silver just like this one. Lucky I came out alive."

"Your fault? Under the influence?"

"My fault. Didn't see that the lane disappeared and there was a wall instead, and I hit it and the car flipped and landed on the roof."

We put the seatbelts on and he pulled out slowly. "I can't see onto the road. Someone might hit me."

"Not in this gentle city! I could step out and signal to you."

I did, and then we drove. He didn't dare switch lanes, looked over his shoulder, not trusting the mirrors, and I looked as well.

"The traffic is actually pretty good. I thought it would be wild, but it's no worse than in Zagreb," I said.

"That's not much comfort. You got to watch out."

He seemed to drive in the wrong gear, in fourth up the hill, losing momentum, and then in first down the hill, grinding, and he was aware of it. "The gear is not as important as the other cars and lampposts. I don't want to hit anything."

"True, but you might not want to burn out the transmission either."

"Don't say that. I am nervous enough."

"I can see that."

"Don't say that. I am!"

He skirted the very edge of the road, nearly scraping the car against the knee-high sidewall.

"You do have a bit more room on the left, you know," I said. "Do you want me to drive? I've driven in Milan, Paris, Frankfurt, Budapest, New York, Moscow . . ."

"No, I am all right. It just takes a few minutes to get used to driving again. And I am self-conscious. You are like a driving inspector."

"So, this fish restaurant. Where is it?"

"Just on the other side of the Danube. Dunavski Pirat."

I admired the views, left and right, of the Danube, the river I knew very well from my days in Budapest and Novi Sad, even broader and larger here, after receiving the waters of the rivers Sava and Tisza. On the left, the white suspension bridge shone above barges filled with coal. Though it was only early April, shades of green already dominated both sides of the river.

"Well, we are here on the other side of the river," I said once we'd crossed. "Can you exit somewhere?"

"Not the first exit. It's tricky. I remember that."

He exited two kilometres later. We drove along the highway and came to the restaurant. Timidly he parked, afraid he might scrape the cars, and then we both stepped out and walked past lacquered red brick walls into the restaurant full of huge taxidermic masterpieces of catfish, pike-perch, carp, and even a shark. We chose a table outside, above the bank of the river, next to a barky oak tree that rose through the roof from the middle of the porch. The sides of the porch were all done in pine, with large open windows. We ordered fish *paprikash* soup, pike-perch and catfish, and *shopska salata* (Bulgarian-style salad).

"What kind of wine would you like?" Mile asked. "In this hot weather and with river fish, I think white would be good."

"Oh, reds are always better. You don't have to listen to TV-cooking-show recommendations."

"It's common sense. Red wine can make you tense, and we both have high blood pressure, I assume?"

"Correct. For that, the best thing to do would be to eat a couple of apples now, and call it quits. But that's not what we are doing, is it?"

"You are right. Let's have a jug of red."

Soon the waiter brought us a large earthenware carafe as though we were in Georgia or Mesopotamia. Mile slurped the red fish *paprikash* soup. The fish, also in large earthenware, was delicious, olive-oiled and garlicked and a bit over-salted—of course over-salted, what food isn't in the Balkans? The view of the Danube was obscured because the plastic sheets that were up as mosquito netting had accumulated a sooty sheen from the river traffic.

"You wouldn't believe the mosquitos along the river," he said.

"I would. I'd rather have a clear view and itch a bit than to . . . I mean, what's the point of sitting riverside if you can't see the glorious river?"

"You see it. You don't need to see all the details. Just imagine you are near-sighted and that's what the river would look like."

"Good point. It's sometimes good not to see the details. Life is more beautiful without them."

"Life. What is life? Everybody talks about it, but it's too big to be talked about."

Mile leaned back in his chair. I'd never paid attention to the colour of his eyes, and their blueness surprised me. With red cheeks belying his old-fashioned vigour, their blue stood out.

"This restaurant is fine," he said, "but they have raised the prices brazenly. I could run a better restaurant and my dishes would be more authentic at half the price. Anyway, let's go to my place."

"How will I make it to Belgrade early in the morning?"

"I'll drive you."

"But if we get drunk, as no doubt we will, we'll oversleep, and my meeting, one of the reasons why I am in Belgrade for the second time in two months, will not take place, and I'll never publish a book in Belgrade, which is a shame, considering I published in the zone, Budapest, Sofia, Warsaw, Moscow, Istanbul . . . even Zagreb."

"Don't be so pessimistic. People will love you here. You kind of fit in with your temperament."

"What do you mean by that?"

He moaned rhetorically.

"Anyway, I paid for a good hotel, and I snore at night, so it will be most peaceful if I go there and we can meet again downtown tomorrow afternoon."

"Forget it. You still haven't seen my vineyard, and haven't tasted my wine. And I want to show you where I plan to make a restaurant. I have a whole building I am not using for anything."

"That's amazing."

"And I have ten thousand litres of wine, mostly white wine, first-rate, organic, and all I need now is dishes. You know, that's easy. You just buy some meat and toss it on the grill and slice tomatoes and onions . . . a hot pepper here and there. But wine? That takes work and love, and time, years."

"I can see that. With your robust body frame, you could inspire confidence as a proprietor."

"Yes, I'd tell the customers I was the chef, but an elderly couple, my friends, would cook. They wouldn't charge much and they would be grateful."

"Maybe in the beginning. Nobody is grateful in the end."

"I am not planning the end. No exit strategy."

"So what's the theme? You have to have some angle for a new restaurant, especially in the boonies. How will you attract the paying customers from Belgrade?"

"They love going a bit sideways, and so we have the floats on

164

the Sava, which are a huge success, even though they are far out in Zemun and Novi Beograd."

"Yes, the theme is floats. Wild stuff. And yours?"

"*Staroslavenska kuhinja*. Old Slavic cuisine."

"Slavic? Are Serbs pan-Slavs? Maybe they used to be, but now, you've had a falling out with just about everybody—Croats, Slovenes, Macedonians, Montenegrins . . . not to mention your old friends the Bulgarians, two fucking Balkan wars. When are you going to have the third one with them?"

"I know. Old Serbian cuisine."

"What is that?"

"I am going to explore it. Maybe hire some ethnographic historian. But basically, you know, mutton, pork, vegetable stews, beans, sour cream and garlic, lots of beans."

"Blood sausages?"

"Now you are teasing me. Anyway, when we think ethnic cuisine, we usually assume only a few dishes, as though our ancestors had no imagination and ate the same thing over and over again, without experimenting, combining, and being inspired. I'll run the kitchen in the spirit of the old Slavic cuisine."

"Serbian, you mean. How about Ungaro-Croato-Serb?"

"Yes, naturally, cuisine was always fusion."

A black and white cat rubbed against my ankles, and stood on his hind legs, sniffing the catch.

"He's well trained," I said. "Not jumping on the table, yet not afraid of people. The right amount of love and fear."

"One thing, it's not safe to eat bony fish when drunk," he said. "You might get needles in your throat."

"Do you have a cat at home?"

"I don't feel good," he said.

"What do you mean? Great food, good wine, mediocre company, you should feel great," I said.

"By mediocre, you don't mean yourself?"

"Yes."

"Oh, we could play with words, but my friend, I don't feel well. I feel tension in my chest, not enough air, and pain around my heart."

"Do you take pills for blood pressure?"

"Yes. Some diuretics and something else."

"A beta blocker?"

"Not a beta blocker. Ace-something. Nitrates. Not sure, I just believe the doctors and swallow."

"What's your pulse like now?"

"I don't know."

"You measure it like this. Put two fingers on the radial side of your wrist, inside, gently, and feel for the beat."

"I can't find it."

"Or on the neck in front of the biggest front neck muscles."

"I can't find it. Maybe my heart is too weak to beat right."

"Don't be silly," I said. "Of course you have a pulse. Give me your hand."

I found his pulse and counted 85 a minute.

"That's not too fast, though a large animal like you should have a slower pulse. Tell you what, I have a beta blocker on me, a small dose, 50 mg of metoprolol. The usual dose is 100. Take it and you'll feel better. It will slow your heart rhythm and lower your pressure."

"Really? But I've never taken it."

"That's fine. It's a tranquilizer. It's used to eliminate physiological side effects of stage fright. Pianists use it. I think you had too much excitement today, driving from Novi Sad, and then all over Belgrade."

He looked suspiciously at the Aspirin-like tablet.

"Also, drink a lot of water, and breathe deep and slow."

He drank water, and breathed slowly.

"You studied medicine. You learned something?"

"I dropped out before I could learn anything clinical, but I would have made a good doctor, that's what my anatomy professor said. I do have the intuition and common sense of one. And I follow research."

"You sure the pill won't do more harm than good?"

"Ninety-six per-cent positive."

Mile opened his mouth like a dog short of breath, and he looked redder than before. His hand stopped halfway across the table. I guess he weighed up the two fears—heart attack and the unreliable pill from an old Croatian friend, friend but Croatian nevertheless. Could he really trust me? Maybe I was sent to poison him?

He looked me in the eye, not blinking, like a huge St. Bernard puppy in distress, looking at a bear. I could see he treated the pill as some kind of explosive, and he calculated, probably, which factor was more important here—that I was an old friend, or that I was a Croatian with resentments about the Serbian destruction of Croatia in the '90s. Serbs kill their political opponents the old-fashioned way, with bullets in hotel lobbies, while Russians and Croats use radioactive chemicals and drugs.

All such potential thoughts and doubts and suspicions only made him tenser and redder, and threatened his heart further. His heart had become his enemy, and he could trust it less than me, I imagined, as we held the gaze, and the fear in his eyes grew, not of me anymore, but of himself.

Who knows what he thought, but it seems the fear of the heart attack prevailed and he took the pill and swallowed, his Adam's apple bobbing as though he were swallowing a whole plum rather than a pill five millimetres in diameter.

"There you go. It will help."

"Now I probably shouldn't drink any wine," he said.

"Yes, it's better not to. It's all mine now!"

He looked at me sombrely and sadly and breathed fast. I imagined that he may have thought about how sad it all was, that friends when tested could not be trusted, that our ethnic histories weighed so heavily between us, like the humidity in the air on this prematurely hot and muggy day, behind the soot-smudged plastic mosquito screen, which prevented fresh air flow.

"Mile, deepen your breath. You need to calm your system. And the more oxygen you have in your blood, the less your heart has to work."

"I don't want to calm it too much."

"Don't worry, your heart won't stop. You aren't going to have a heart attack."

"How do you know?"

"True, I don't. Most heart attacks take place in the morning, early in the morning."

"The humidity messes with me and exhausts me."

"Me too. It's normal. Once it rains, you'll be all dandy; this is just a bit of atmospheric pressure, you are right about that. You know what, let's not obsess or you will drive yourself insane."

"I am insane."

"Let's keep eating. The fish will be cold."

We ate. I gave the fish's head to the cat. It purred and crunched the bones. Mile also gave the cat his fish's head. "Smart cat," he said. "Chose the right place to be."

"Yes, I'd say if I had a choice between being a bookstore cat or a fish restaurant cat, I'd choose the fish place."

He chewed with his eyes closed, and a tear showed up in the corner of his eyes. I wondered whether he got a bone in his throat.

"Now tell me more about your restaurant idea," I said. "Will you have fish?"

"Of course, only river fish as we are too far from the sea. And rabbit, goose, duck, venison, boar."

"You know that the Papuk Mountain is now the best boar-hunting area in the world. Even Russians come there to hunt."

"I know. That's what happens when you lose all the Serbian hunters!"

"Croatia has gone to the pigs now. Wild pigs."

"Sometimes I dream of hunting in those mountains," he said.

"A friend of mine does. After the war, he had a grenade launcher in his garage, and he fired into a herd of boars, killing seven of them."

"That sounds like a tall tale."

"Wouldn't put it past Darko. You know him, the tall bony guy with a large broken nose, boxer-style."

Mile kept chewing slowly, with his eyes closed, and didn't answer.

"Well, it's been more than 20 minutes since you took the beta blocker. It should begin to take effect. Do you feel any better?"

"I wish I could tell you did. I am dizzy. I think it would be hard for me to stand up. If I did, I'd probably fall."

He looked at me, and I didn't reply. I worried. What if he actually gets worse, has a heart attack, goes to a hospital, and tells the doctors I gave him a beta blocker, and it turns out that with his kind of heart failure, that's the last thing he should take. With an atrophied distended heart—if that's the case with him—a beta blocker could actually precipitate a heart attack or, even more likely, a stroke, with the slowing of the blood flow. Shit. So if he gets to the hospital, they will ask him what he took, and he could say a beta blocker from a Croatian friend, and I could be arrested. And suppose he dies, I'll be charged with murder.

Now I looked at him with my own large panicked eyes, and I felt heat in my cheeks, partly from the red wine and the heat, but even more from my thoughts. The mind can poison even the skin, let alone the heart. What if my tension gets me? I'd forgotten to take blood pressure pills all day.

Of course, I should worry more about him than about me.

Wouldn't it be amazing, I thought, if we both had heart attacks in the restaurant, assassinated by our own minds?

"Wait a second," I said, and took out 100 mgs of metoprolol and began to swallow it. I chased it with wine—not the prescriptive method. "Do you smoke?"

"I did, until a year go."

"Are you better?"

"How could I be better in a hurry?"

We kept eating in silence. We both had our thoughts spinning and affecting us. If he stopped thinking, I bet he would be all right. And maybe if I stopped thinking and projecting my anxieties and fears, he would feel more relaxed and better too, less threatened.

"By the way, how was it to work as a bouncer in Zagreb?" I asked him, out of the blue, partly to take our minds elsewhere. After all, we always had our past over which to reminisce, more past than we had future to speculate on. If we could pull through the next hour, we'd be all right.

"Oh, it was wonderful," he replied. "You know it was the late seventies, the American sexual revolution had reached us, nobody worried about STDs, people got drunk, and hot girls sometimes led me into the dark passage at the side of the club, and we'd grope, sometimes have a quickie, some nights three or four, so it got to be exhausting. Oh, those were the days!"

"You didn't seem to be interested in girls before going to Zagreb."

"I was just shy. Didn't know how to express interest, but in the club, I didn't have to. Girls whose boyfriends passed out on brandy would come up to me. Strange enough, before that, I never liked the idea of blowjobs, but I got more of them than I could remember, and it was heavenly. I got addicted then. You know, sex is a powerful drug. My mind is still diseased with it, but now it's all mental."

"As you are not married, you can . . ."

"Actually, I am. But to tell you the truth, this blood pressure, heart, and so on, well, I haven't done it in a while. Strange how life is—if I could have distributed the action I had as a young man over my lifespan, it would be just right. Now the few times I get together with a strange woman, I have to worry whether I can get it up, so it's no fun, it's just embarrassing. Before, it was just a thoughtless delight, and now it's like a medical exam."

"You are married and you never mentioned your wife."

"That's how it goes. Once you are married for a long time, what's there to say? I am not proud of being married."

"Clearly."

"I wouldn't be proud of being single either. Maybe it would be harder. Anyway, I married a gazelle and live with a bear. That's the fate of us in the Balkans. And women can say, I married a panther, and I live with a boar. Most of my friends complain of what's become of their marriages."

"So you are feeling better now?"

"Yes, I feel better, still a little dizzy, and tired from the atmospheric pressure, bad heart."

"Maybe the beta blocker is helping after all."

"Maybe."

The bill came. Four thousand dinars.

"Now that's not helping," he said. "My God, this is armed robbery. This place used to be earthy and cheap but now . . ."

"Well, it's not all that bad, sixty dollars."

"It's like one-sixth of many people's salaries."

"Don't worry, I'll cover it."

"You are my guest. I'll pay, of course."

"No, I'll pay."

I expected a long and protracted battle, which I would lose because that is how things used to be in Belgrade thirty years ago. Serbian friends were proud and competitive hosts.

I took out 4,400 dinars and put the paper money into the little basket in which the bill sat, written in slanted Cyrillic.

"Thank you," he said. "You didn't have to. And now let's go to my place, and I'll treat you to some really fine wines, my labour of love."

I was a little taken aback that I had won this bill-paying session just as I had a couple of months before when I had visited Belgrade as well. I won all the bill-paying duels. And he offered wine as his contribution to the bill, somehow.

"It's already pretty late, after nine. I'd rather go to my hotel, and maybe we can do the wine-tasting tomorrow or the day after."

"As you wish. But it would be much better now, we are practically already there, only five kilometres away, and by now, almost twenty away from your hotel."

"Well, you know, I woke up very early to get here, and the quiet of the hotel before my work tomorrow would do me good. This was great, and to be continued."

"But it would be better if you visited. Now is now, and who knows if we will ever get a chance again."

"Oh, how you talk. You are fine."

He drove unsteadily, and nearly hit the curb and then over-reacted into the other lane.

What the hell? I thought. Is he having a heart attack right now? I reached out to grab the wheel. He steadied the driving, and I put the hand back in my lap.

We came to the main road, and he lingered at the stop sign, idling, the car sliding a bit back, and then, obviously in third gear, he started forward to correct the backslide, and the car stalled at the crossing before he could turn left to cross the Danube back into Belgrade.

He hesitated a little, gasped, and restarted the engine, grinding it with the key turned too long.

"You know how to find the address?"

"I kind of do. But I don't feel well. Fuck it, I can't breathe."

"Maybe you should see a doctor."

"It's late. I don't know where to find one now."

"ER at the nearest hospital."

"I don't know where . . . And I don't want emergencies."

He gasped and looked terrified, his thick eyebrows arched high and white, and he groaned.

I wondered: is he just faking a heart attack so he wouldn't have to drive to Belgrade? I thought it was his beloved town, and look how he fears it. Maybe he's been playing all evening long, just to get out of the chore of driving through the lively traffic? That's probably it, he's an excellent actor after all, and he wants to get his way, and what is his way? To get me to visit him at home, to show me how well he's doing, and what a great host he is. Now how bad is that? And why am I stuck on protecting my prepaid reservation of seventy-five dollars? It's done, and I can sleep at the hotel, and the seventy-five will be gone, or I can sleep at my friend's place, and the seventy-five will be gone? What's the difference? I should just count my losses, and fuck him, faking or not, he doesn't mean ill. Even if I were to lose seventy-five more dollars, who cares, is friendship a price tag?

"Fuck it," I said. "I don't want to jeopardize your health. This drive—even the thought of it—seems to be killing you. Let's just go to your place and I'll crash there."

"Oh good, thank you!"

He turned to the right. His driving improved instantly.

"Pancevo is pretty sleepy, I guess," I said. "Where is the big glass factory?"

"It shut down."

"Really? It was the largest one in Yugoslavia."

"I think you are right. Anyway, those chimneys in the dark over there, that's where it used to be."

"It's great to see it. My father did contract work for them. You have no idea how often I thought of this place, and how much, even as a kid, I worked to send wooden shoes here. Sometimes I stayed up all nights with my father, at the age of nine and ten, nailing leather onto wooden soles, and then I carted the large hemp sacks, fifty pairs per sack, to the train station before dawn, sometimes ten trips, to deliver to the cargo train, addressed simply, Staklana, Pancevo, SFR Srbija. The factory workers couldn't walk around the hot floors in rubber shoes, and the wooden clogs provided the best insulation, the workers loved them. Oh, this means a lot to me." I gazed into the dark and the still chimneys in the moonlight. "Obliquely, I have more roots here than you do," I said.

"No doubt," he replied.

We took another turn to the right—most of our turns, somehow, were to the right—and in a couple of kilometres, he said, "Here we are!"

He pulled into the crunchy driveway. He showed me his bread brick-oven, containing two floors and windows, with the chimney two stories high, large enough to bake and grill sheep, pigs, and oxen if need be, and then he led me down the stairs into his dank wine cellar. We bent our heads, and I waved off a sticky cobweb from my eyebrows.

"Here I have three thousand bottles of white wine. I have another cellar with seven thousand more." He stood, proud, showing his produce.

I met his wife—she was not all that bulky after all—whose eyes shone, and she said, "I heard a lot about you!" I met his mother-in-law next, a classic Balkan widow all in black, who immediately offered us walnut strudel.

"Oh, thank you, you wouldn't believe how stuffed we got at Dunavski Pirat," I said.

"But Mile, why?" his mother-in-law asked. "Oh, these young people these days. They don't know how to host."

She inquired after my lineage, and knew my older brother who, as a doctor, used to treat her three decades before, for rheumatism of the knees.

Mile showed me the house. "See, I had it built to measure. I drew the plan. I like plenty of open space, and high ceilings and arches."

"Good design," I said.

"People think I am lazy, and I can be. I spent the last year sitting and thinking about what to do with my life, sunbathing on the terrace, shirtless. But see, I have my spells of work. Let's go to the porch and have some wine. Riesling, similar to what we have in Western Slavonia, and Pinot Grigio."

"I saw pictures of you hiking in Italy," I said. "Is that where you fell in love with Grigio?"

"You got it. Now, tell me which one you like better."

I tasted the wines. "They are both great, but it would be better if they were chilled. I think Riesling is more interesting, fruitier."

"Yes, I know. I've put a couple of bottles into the freezer, but for now we'll make do with these."

"With pleasure. It's really fantastic, so pure tasting."

"I know. I get organic grapes, or as close to it as possible. My vineyard doesn't yield enough, so I have to buy. You know, they always spray some, they have to in this moist region. And what does organic in our filthy world mean?"

"Of course."

"I put in no additives, no sulphates, and you'll see, you won't get a hangover from this, no matter how much you drink."

"That sounds ominous."

"Yes, it is. Very ominous!"

We toasted. *Zivili,* and looked each other in the eyes, holding the gaze. I read somewhere that in India you are supposed to hold the gaze while drinking tea as long as your sip lasts, and I took that to be a good principle for wine: as long as my gulp took, that's how long my gaze should hold.

The clouds created a black layer above the dusky sky, and then again above the fields. In the distance, they rumbled.

"Obviously, it has to rain soon," I said.

"I hope so."

A yellow three-legged dog hopped by, below the cement porch.

"He's bumming for food, but we are not eating. People sometimes drop off their puppies here. It would be better if they neutered their dogs like the Americans do. Go away, shhh, sss," he hissed at the dog, and threw a rotten apple after him.

"Aren't you sorry for the poor creature?"

"He's a pest. I can't afford to feel sorry for them all."

It began to rain. We'd each already finished three glasses, and now he brought out chilled wine. We drank it, our throaty gulps click-clacking like horse hooves on a dusty road far away.

"How is your heart?" I asked.

"Completely fine! All good now."

I laughed, as though he'd told me a wonderful joke, but mostly from relief. Well, most laughter is some kind of relief.

"The rain has relieved the pressure," Mile said. "I really do react to the congestion in the weather by all sorts of congestions in my body."

"Maybe the fact that you've had a litre of wine may have something to do with your sense of well-being?"

We both chuckled, and said, *Zivili*, "To your life," once again. Our language, along with Hebrew and a few other languages, contains this toast, "To Life," or "Live!" We also have *Na zdravlje*, for "Health!" But *Zivili* is more common, and perhaps existential. Health, that may be too much to ask for, but as long as we are alive, it's good, let's live. That's all we can ask for. The toast may have been born out of bad history, who knows, but somehow I always preferred it to toasting health while damaging it.

"So, no doctor tonight?"

"No, maybe tomorrow. I can't guarantee that we'll feel good after two more bottles."

"I am glad I stayed here, to see your fiefdom. It's nice here. And the wine is perfect. I see why you were eager to share it."

"Tomorrow, before we go to Belgrade, I'll show you where I plan to open the restaurant. It's a big building and it's empty."

"How come it's yours?"

"That's all I got from my partnership with two other guys—we had a large coffee company, coffee from Brazil; we got it green, roasted it, and sold both whole and ground beans. It was all fine and started out well, but then Todorovic's large firms suppressed us. We couldn't advertise enough to keep a market share and so, before we went bankrupt, we sold out, and this is all I got."

"Sounds pretty good. And how did you get into the coffee business? You seem to be running it in the wrong order. First wine and then coffee, that would be the right progression."

"I feel so much better! If I could be half-drunk all the time, I don't think I'd have any problems. But you know, it's impossible, I'd get over-drunk, then I have a vicious hangover, and then my heart aches. But just a steady tipsiness, if I had the temperament, the pacing, oh, that would be the life!"

"I agree. You know, after a few drinks, your blood pressure actually goes down. It's only in hangovers and later on that it goes up."

"Why is that? If wine relaxes us, the relaxation should last."

"That's a mystery. It doesn't make sense that drinking overall should raise blood pressure, since at the time you are actually drinking, it lowers it. Whatever, *Zivili!*"

The rain became intense, and the chill air cleansed and soothed our skins, lungs, and hearts. Pine and cypress aromas rode on the raindrops in heavenly luxury.

"You know," I said, "our wine drinking and this rain remind me of how I tried to raise my son religiously, so when he was four years old, I read to him Old Testament stories, simplified for children. He liked the Noah story—the naughty people drank too much wine, and God, in anger, decided to flood the earth. So, once I visited an old friend, with whom I drank wine; my son begged me to stop, afraid there would be a flood. Next day, on our drive to New Jersey, it rained so intensely that we had to stop before a deep flooded section of the road—I decided to go through, and the water came up to the windows. Luckily, we were not swept away but pulled through, while he shrieked in the back seat, thinking this was the end."

"Nice story!" Mile said. "Let's toast to it!"

We kept drinking until we were groggy.

We went to sleep with our windows open, and sooner than I was ready for it, Mile woke me up. "What kind of coffee would you like?" he asked. He wasn't as ruddy as the evening before, but a bit ashen and pained. "It's too early," he said, "but I promised."

"Turkish. What time is it?"

"Nine. Your meeting's at 10? We'll make it. Where?"

"Hotel Balkan."

"Yes, Hotel Balkan," he echoed, as though it meant something extra.

We drove over the bridge in a drizzle, and the greys dominated the greens on the banks of the river. Mile drove excellently, without any hesitant moves, and inspired so much confidence that I didn't look over his shoulder as he switched lanes.

"This evening, come to my place, and we'll bake something good, a goose maybe, and drink more."

"Tomorrow night would be better."

We shook hands, and said, Okay, *vidimo se prekosutra*. See you the day after tomorrow.

During my meeting with a Serbian publisher, the publisher said, "You think I am a publisher? There's no more publishing. People have no money, they don't read, or if they do, they borrow books from friends, ten copies sell, it's not a business, I now run an advertising agency and organize a festival, and primarily I write, I write novels now. And this is a horrible country, full of backstabbers and liars and thieves and fascists, I don't know what you want from us, fuck us, it's all gone to hell. I hate the place, oh, I love the city, but I hate what's become of it, the sheer vandalism, the death of book culture, I know, it's worldwide, but it's worse here...."

He gushed for two hours his resentment for his homeland, and I didn't have the heart to put my books in his hands, and I paid for our four coffees, and we shook hands, and promised to stay in touch, do some kind of international festival, maybe in Sarajevo. And later in the day, I saw the woman I used to be in love with as a 14-year-old, now my age. She'd been the source of so much longing and heartache, and I could barely recognize her. She'd grown heavy and rough, wearing thick glasses, and talked only about disease, mostly cancers in Belgrade and Western Slavonia, and who died of what, and in the end, she said, "You haven't changed," and I said, "Thank you, that's impossible," and as I leaned over to kiss her cheek goodbye, the visor of my baseball cap scraped her.

And later, I stayed at the prepaid reservation hotel (this one downtown, down the hill from the Presidential Palace), and went downstairs to a jazz bar, and watched the tail end of Real Madrid winning the Spanish cup against Barcelona, and two tall, elegant girls danced and looked over their shoulders at me, somehow invitingly, but I had no more cash left to treat them to drinks, and thought it would be embarrassing just to talk and have nothing to offer, and so I kept looking at Modric passing the ball to Benzema, on the screen, and later when I went to my room, I wished I had the vitality and sprightliness and the courage to be with the young ladies, who looked too good to be true, but then, shouldn't the truth be good-looking and beautiful? So maybe it was all true, but I stepped out of the truth into my room, and actually wished I were drinking with Mile on his cypress-scented porch. After all, we were friends. I slept at his place and drank his wine, and I was not even hungover, let alone poisoned, and it never crossed my mind to mistrust him. Maybe it never crossed his mind to mistrust me—I had imagined him being suspicious. But who knows what's bothering him, after all. How to know? I don't understand anyone, not even myself.

The rain that had started during our drinking the night before wouldn't relent, and it rained for days, until the whole region flooded, and people grew depressed, and so did Mile. I called Mile two days after our meeting, and he said, "Eh, my friend, this rain is getting to me. I have no will to do anything, and my heart feels heavy and crumpled, like it's made of rust. How long are you staying? Let's roast a suckling pig when the rain is over."

"All right, let's do that."

I left the town before the rainfall ended, only three days after getting to Belgrade, and ate an oily and sour burek as the bus pulled out of the terminal, spraying muddy water out of the potholes onto the empty sidewalk.

Café Sarajevo

In the Balkans, nothing vanishes completely. In my hometown, people give directions like this: You go two blocks past the oil refinery, and then one block up, past the military barracks, and then turn left. . . . The oil refinery shut down a long time ago, as have the barracks, but in people's minds it's all still there. For a newcomer it's maddening, but for the people who call it home, perhaps it's comforting to use, in the midst of all the changes, the map of the old town, from fifty years ago. The old town is still stronger than the new one.

In the New World, in North America, it's very different. So many new buildings come up that we quickly forget about the old ones that used to be there. In Montreal, the new impressive Sports Station bar has just opened up, and Café Sarajevo has vanished, and nobody seems to notice or comment. Sarajevo used to be a large café with a Balkan mix of music, à la Bregovic, and burek, baklava, and many other Bosnian delicacies. I hung out there a few times and when choosing a neighbourhood in which to live, I decided I would move there, St. Laurent, a little north of Bernard, before the gates of Little Italy.

When I moved into my new place, I walked out and where there used to be Café Sarajevo, there was an open floor with large glass windows, and the red sign for Sarajevo was gone, and the windows bore an "*À louer*" sign, taped and slanted.

Most of my friends didn't seem to notice—there's a wealth of cafés in the area: Bethlehem, a Peruvian fish restaurant, the Vices & Versa brew pub, Odessa coffee shop, Le Vieux Vélo.

Not far from me on St. Hubert Street, there was a Balkan bakery, and once I ate a burek from it, but when I got to the store, it had closed down for good as well. On St. Laurent, next to the former Café Sarajevo, there was Café Adria. I had expected it to be Croatian, but when I spoke in Croatian to the customers there, they were not pleased, and they informed me they were from Serbia. They could have been pleased, but that's just it, after the war, you never know how people will react. Perhaps that's why our ethnic restaurants and cafés close down in communities where there aren't huge numbers of us. There aren't enough of us, of a single ethnicity, and we don't have a pan-ethnic ex-Yugoslav community to maintain a Balkan café. Quantity amounts to quality, to use the maxim of dialectical materialism, and there just aren't enough of us.

Yet not all the regional traces of Balkan immigrants have vanished. Around the corner from Bernard, on Clark, there's a Slovenian butcher's, Slovenia, with a mélange of smoked meats and sausages, sort of a cross between Austria and Hungary and the Balkans. There's another Slovenian deli farther down on St. Laurent, and a bakery called Pekarna on St. Catherine, but it hardly has any Slovenian flavour left, other than the name and walnut and poppy-seed rolladas.

Maybe our people can't keep an establishment going, but they are still all over the city, and I hear their voices in passing. And that's more important to me. I still see Café Sarajevo and Adria as I walk around. It's not so much about the walls as it is about the people. For example, while watching a Djokovic-Federer tennis match at the Sports Station on St. Catherine Street, I met a man in a leather jacket with brown hair combed straight up, on the sidewalk, looking in. His name was Branko. He didn't want to come in, but preferred to watch from the sidewalk so he could smoke. And moreover, he said, he feared any kind of enclosure.

Afterwards, I kept running into him all over the city—on St. Catherine, on Bernard, in Westmount — and I wondered how come he walked so much, or was he shadowing me? Now, with the people from our region, it's easy to grow paranoid, as we were trained in paranoia under communism, believing there were spies everywhere, and the war didn't improve that attitude.

So I asked Branko to explain his omnipresence.

"It's a walking syndrome," he said.

He offered me a flask of French brandy, Chateaubriand, the cheapest, but pretty good.

"By the way, what's your ethnicity?" I asked him.

"Only peasants and fascists ask such a crude question."

"It's not rude, just curiosity. Even if I didn't ask you, I would wonder. You don't want me to be a hypocrite, do you? You probably wonder what nationality I am."

"No, you sound Croatian, but you could be Serbian; I have no idea, and I don't care. It doesn't matter what nationality you are, only that you drink well, and that you are not a bad drunk. Have a sip!" He pushed the flask toward me.

"No, I don't drink at the moment," I said.

"Oh Jesus, don't tell me you're a born-again North American prude."

"So why do you walk so much? I admire the fact that you can."

"Yes, it's healthy," he said, "but I am restless, I can't be still very long. I was trapped so long during the siege of Sarajevo that now I must walk outdoors; I have fear of entrapment."

"Really? But you were a Serb in Sarajevo."

"Why do you say that?"

"Well, you root for Djokovic."

"Come on, I also root for the Croatian national soccer team. But all right, if you insist. Sure, O.K., but that didn't matter once you were trapped in the city. Grenades and shrapnel don't ask for your ID."

"Why the hell didn't you leave? And didn't you know this was coming? In my hometown, Serbs knew there would be a Serbian siege, so most of them left."

"But not all? Well, that was the case in Sarajevo. I didn't believe any of the crap I was hearing. I thought it was just hate talk, so I didn't leave. And then I was stuck. There was no way out unless you had special connections with the UN."

"What did you do in Sarajevo?"

"I was an opera singer."

To substantiate his story, he took a good swig of brandy, and sang several arias. He stood straight, and gesticulated, and threw back his somewhat balding head, to look up high. He sounded good. When he talked you would never guess he had an operatic voice, as his voice was kind of subdued and damaged.

"Everything went to hell during the siege, even my voice," he said.

"So how do you live here?"

"I came as an exile and war invalid. They call it a post-traumatic stress disorder. It's not a disorder, to my mind. If you went through what I went through, you'd be crazy not to be disturbed. Fifteen grenades hit my apartment on different occasions, and I had to spend weeks in the basement in the dark. I'd want to see how these guys who like to call my mental state disordered would take it."

"But it's all right to be an invalid. They support you."

"The Canadian government gives me enough for rent and thirty dollars a day for food."

"That's not bad."

"You try eating and drinking on thirty a day. Not complaining. But the damned cigarettes cost ten bucks. And look at this." He pointed to the tree. "It's the seventh of May, and the leaves are not out yet. I heard in Sarajevo they were all out in February. It was a horrible winter."

"But you are holding out. Why not go back? You know, I visited Sarajevo, stayed on Ljubljanska across the Potok Bridge, toward Grbavica."

"That's the bridge I used to escape. I had to pay 5000DM, and I left one year before the siege was over. You know what they call the bridge now? Romeo and Juliet. At the beginning of the siege, a couple wanted to run across it, to escape to Dubrovnik. He was a Serb and she was Muslim. Snipers got them in the middle of the bridge and they lay there for three days and nights, and nobody dared pick them up because the snipers covered the whole range. So we watched the bodies from a distance."

I showed him some pictures on the laptop from Sarajevo, a pavement near the Croatian cathedral, marked in red, to comemorate victims of a grenade.

"I stood right there, on that spot, one day," he said, "after a bomb fell up the hill and killed several dozen people. The stream of blood was an inch thick, covering the heels of my shoes. So now you see why I couldn't walk there again."

"Hum. So when is Novak Djokovic playing again?"

"See you later, brother," he said. "And you know, if you walk enough, you will."

Several days later I walked down on Bernard Street and I thought I saw him. I didn't. But his presence is strong in my mind; wherever I go, he could appear, and even if he doesn't, he's there.

CREDITS

These stories appeared in the following publications:

"Tumbling: Belgrade," *Narrative Magazine*; "Tumbleweed," *American Fiction* VII, and the current version in *Matrix*; "Easy Living," *The Land Grant College Review*; "Strings," *Exile Quarterly* and *Literal Latte*; "My Hairs Stood Up," *Gulf Coast Review*; "Tumbling: Daruvar," *The Southern Review*; "Byeli: The Definitive Biography of a Nebraskan Tomcat," *The New England Review/Bread Loaf Quarterly*; "Stalin's Perspective," *Prairie Schooner; Distinguished Essay, Best American Essays*; "Son of a Gun," *Witness Magazine, Distinguished Essay, Best American Essays*; "Tumbling: Maine," *The Southern Review*; "Zidane the Ram," *St. Petersburg Review*; "A Cat Named Sobaka," *Prairie Schooner, Lasche Award, Distinguished Essay, Best American Essays*; "Putin's Dry Law," *Prick of the Spindle*; "Crossbar," *Guernica*, anthologized in *Zagreb Noir*; "Tumbling: Croatia," *Prick of the Spindle*; "Prepaid Reservation," *Exile Quarterly Review*; "Café Sarajevo," *Flaneur Magazine*.

ACKNOWLEDGEMENTS

I would like to thank the editors of the journals for publishing the stories, and in many cases, helping me shape them. And I'd like to especially thank editor Dimitri Nasrallah for collecting these stories together, and Simon Dardick for valiantly publishing them. Thanks also to John Goldbach, Jeanette Novakovich, Bükem Reitmeyer, and Tim O'Brien for reading some of the early versions of the stories.

I am grateful for the time to bum around and work that several agencies have provided me with: The New York Public Library Dorothy and Lewis B. Cullman Center for Scholars and Writers; Black Mountain Institute at UNLV; the Hermitage Artists Retreat in Florida; Yaddo; the Canada Council for the Arts; the Fulbright Commission; the Norton Island Residency, and the Concordia University Centre for Research and Development.